PLAY to WIN

G★ME
Changers

A.C. ARTHUR

AN ARTISTRY PUBLISHING BOOK
PLAY TO WIN, First Edition: 2020
Copyright © 2020 by A.C. Arthur
All rights reserved.
Cover Art Design © 2020 by Croco Designs

This book is a work of fiction. Characters, names, locations, events and incidents (in either a contemporary and/or historical setting) are products of the author's imagination and are being used in an imaginative manner as a part of this work of fiction. Any resemblance to actual events, locations, settings or persons, living or dead, is entirely coincidental.

www.acarthur.net

A fifteen-year-old Ethan Henley would have thought he'd died and gone to sexual heaven. Thirty-one-year-old Ethan wasn't far off that mark himself.

The sounds were distinctive. *Oohs* and *ahhs* that only came during the throes of pleasure. Or at least he was almost certain of that fact, as he walked down a wide hallway at the Regional Resort and Spa in Alexandria. It was Friday night and just a couple of hours ago, he'd been ready to leave Game Changers, the sports bar he co-owned with five of his closest friends, when a call from Rodney Hankin, a regular at the bar, came in. Rodney needed a favor. One that could lead to referrals from Rodney to other men having bachelor parties, to use Game Changers instead of the new upscale resort. That was the only reason Ethan agreed to drive just outside the town of Providence, Virginia, where he lived, to make this delivery.

This resort had opened just a few weeks ago and as far as he'd heard, was living up to all the grand hype they'd seen on television. That meant the resort was probably charging a small fortune for that huge conference room Rodney and twenty other guys were occupying right now.

If that were the case, he wondered how much whoever was in the room just ahead was paying to have sex in this new fancy facility.

Ethan's booted feet were silent on the gold and blue carpet, his ears tuned to the now undeniable, "Yeah, baby!" he heard next.

Without further thought, he was already turning slightly to the right toward the partially open door with the sign that read "Blow Jobs 101". His dick throbbed. The words, mixed with the sounds made him even more eager to get inside, but he was stopped before taking another step.

"Excuse me," a woman's voice said from behind.

The interruption wasn't welcome, just as it wouldn't have been if he'd actually been in the middle of a round of hot and sweaty sex. He was already thinking of the odds of making that very thing happen once he left here, because two months had obviously been way too long to go without. Frowning, he turned around.

"You look like you could use a massage, big guy." To say the dark-haired woman standing before him was scantily dressed may have been an understatement.

He hadn't noticed anyone in the hallway before, but now she was standing directly in front of him. She wore only a few strategically placed strings at her waist and between her legs, with stars pasted over her nipples, and she was rubbing her hands down his chest. She was right about one thing, Ethan was a big guy, standing at six feet three inches, two hundred and twenty pounds of sculpted muscle. He towered over the smaller-framed woman.

"No thanks." He grasped her wrists before pushing her gently away from him. Horny or not, he'd never really warmed to the idea of having sex with strangers.

She winked. "They're free until ten, if you change your mind."

In the next seconds, she was gone, walking away from him to approach another man he saw coming through double doors of a space marked "Exhibition Hall". This man was slim, wearing a hooded jacket and dark framed glasses. He smiled at the woman, who was only a few inches taller than him. This time her hands moved further down until she was openly gripping the man's crotch. What the hell kind of event were they having here? This type of action was a definite no-go at Game Changers, but he'd be lying if he said he wasn't interested in learning more about it. Turning his gaze from the couple, he pushed the door in front of him open. Whether he was interested in the woman or not, if he'd continued staring at the little show she and her new man were giving him, Ethan was certain he'd start mimicking some of the same sounds he'd heard coming from this room.

With that thought embarrassingly on his mind, he entered the room only to be surprised that it was full of people. He hadn't known what to expect but it certainly wasn't an audience. Closing the door quietly, he remained in the back. A quick glance around the room told him there were approximately fifty people sitting in chairs that faced the front. The door behind him was the only entrance or exit and there were no windows. Across the room was one hotel employee who was dusting a table that was obviously clean and empty, and a woman with long, curly hair and rose-tinted lips standing at the front. He shook his head as he reminded himself that he was no longer in the Secret Service. Surveying and analyzing who was in the room and the quickest route of escape was no longer necessary.

"This next technique is called the blizzard," the woman standing at the front of the room with the sensual lips said. He couldn't take his eyes off her lips and folded his arms over his chest while continuing to stare like everyone else in the room.

· · ·

"This is pretty messy, but we all know there can be pleasure in the mess." She smiled, and his gut clenched.

The room erupted in laughter and his gaze was momentarily snatched from her. A few guys in the audience were nodding, one woman in the front row even cheered.

"I'll explain it and then I'll demonstrate. You're going to first fill your mouth with whipped cream." Immediately his eyes were back on her, on the bottom lip which was fuller than the top and barest glimpse of her very pink tongue. Swallowing hard was an instinct, gliding his tongue along his bottom lip was a direct result of the images of where he'd like her to put those lips on him flashed in his mind. The crowd quieted, staring forward as if a million dollars were about to be up for grabs.

"Once your mouth is full, you're going to grip the base of his penis. Rub along his balls for a second, just to get him more excited."

She smiled and Ethan felt a quick punch in his gut. He cleared his throat in an effort to convince himself that he was imagining the sudden loss of breath. But as he watched her slim fingers fold around the bottom of a brown dildo, his dick hardened and pulsed.

"Now, once he's squirming on the bed and begging you to hurry up and take him into your mouth, give him what he wants. Take him in completely, keeping one hand at his base. Then you're going to blow out slightly so that the whipped cream leaves your mouth and covers his length. Pull your mouth away quickly and give him a good drizzle of saliva as you stare up at him. Eye contact is key. It says, 'I know what you want and I'm here to give it to you.' So do it. Give it to him," she said, licking her lips.

A couple of men in the front row clapped, one in the back groaned. A few women nodded in agreement as they laughed. Ethan almost came in his jeans.

"Now, I'll show you how it's done."

He didn't know what he'd expected to find coming into this room. He'd only been here to make a beer delivery, not witness… what the hell was he about to witness? His dick was already pressing persistently against his zipper, his body on full alert and expecting some sort of pleasure in return. If this woman actually did what he thought she was about to do, he was definitely going to lose it! Damn, he hoped that wasn't the case. At thirty-one years old, he was too damn old to come at the sight of a woman giving a blow job to a dildo, especially in a room full of people.

In one hand, the woman whose plump lips his gaze was once again fixated upon, retrieved a red can of whipped cream and tilted her head back to squirt some into her open mouth.

Someone from the crowd actually yelled, "Yes!"

Ethan didn't bother looking to see who'd said what, his gaze was locked on her.

After setting the can back on the table, she looked out to the crowd and wiggled her brows—carefully arched brows that sat above expressive eyes. She was too far away for him to note the exact colors of those eyes, but it was still one of the sexiest gestures he'd ever seen. He swallowed hard, again and bit back a curse. Was this really happening and if it was, why the hell couldn't he be in a room alone with this woman? There was no time for an answer because in the next seconds she was lowering her head, mouth open over the dildo. She made a sound, one that said she was totally enjoying what she was doing, and took the entire length of the dildo in, until her lips touched the fingers that were holding it at the base.

This time he blinked to be certain he was seeing exactly what he thought he was seeing. His over-aroused body was certain whatever was going on here was a good thing and pushed him to do something to make it even better.

She pulled back quickly, leaving the whipped cream to drip down the length of the dildo. Ethan sucked in a breath. His dick throbbed painfully, teeth and fingers closed into a tight fist to keep from groaning.

Her tongue twirled as she moved further away, and a trail of whipped cream-filled saliva dripped down onto the tip of the dildo. There was no way he could resist imagining that warm, wet mouth closing around him. He could see those desire-filled eyes staring up at him, plump lips smeared with whipped cream. He would drive his hands into her hair at that point, scraping his fingers along her scalp as he held tightly, guiding her mouth back down to his dick.

The immediate noise from the crowd yanked him from the blissful images in his mind. Everyone in the class came to their feet, clapping, smiling and totally appreciating the demonstration. When she lowered her head once more and took the dildo into her mouth, this time bobbing her head up and down, moaning with pleasure and creating a flurry of whipped cream flakes in the process, applause echoed throughout the room.

Ethan unclenched his fingers, moving one hand slowly and hopefully discreetly, over to cup his rock-hard erection. The action only made him want more. He either needed to find someone to give him head like this or allow him to plunge deep inside her while thinking about another woman. Then there was the most likely scenario, where he blew the speed limit trying to get home so that he could jerk off in a hot shower.

"Fuck!" He cursed quietly because he didn't like any of his options.

But apparently he wasn't as quiet as he thought because when he looked up the crowd had turned in his direction and the instructor—with the sexy lips who now looked strangely familiar—were all staring back at him.

Portia had seen him come in. His tall, broad frame dressed in all black looking like a complicated mix of somber and sexy was hard to miss. He was late. The class had started fifteen minutes ago. She'd had four sessions today and would return to this room at eight tomorrow morning to sign copies of her book, *The Principles of Pleasure,* which had been released a week ago. Her publisher-arranged book tour was starting off with a bang as she participated in the "F" is for Fetish Adult Entertainment Conference. Her schedule for the last two days had been intense, but Portia had to admit she was enjoying every second of it. Until he'd entered the room.

She moved slowly to set the now very messy dildo down on the table. Picking up a napkin, she wiped her hands and mouth, while silently praying her fingers didn't tremble in front of the room full of people. She did all of this before chancing a second look at him.

"Would you like to join me?" she asked and then immediately clamped her lips shut.

That hadn't sounded right.

A few women in the class began to applaud because obviously, it'd sounded just fine to them. Heat infused her cheeks and she struggled to maintain her composure, flashes of her very awkward teenage years appearing in her mind.

As for him—the guy with the great body and aqua green eyes —he slowly moved his hand from his crotch and replied, "No. Thank you."

He continued to stare at her, similar to a time she recalled all too often that had taken place twelve years ago. She'd always loved when he looked at her, even if she'd had no clue what to do about it back then. That heat from her cheeks transferred down to spread throughout her body alerting her to the pleasure she taught for profit, but routinely denied herself.

This wasn't a foreign sensation to her. In fact, she was often aroused by her research and preparations for her classes. It was part of her occupation, just not a very active part of her real life. Yet, this time was different. This time the arousal was more intense, more urgent and much more intimate than any of her lessons and she knew why.

Ethan Henley. The guy who'd occupied all her teenage dreams until that fateful day when they'd come face-to-face, and he'd rejected her just as her parents and all the other kids in the pitiful town of Providence had done.

"Okay." She paused and cleared her throat. "Let's get back to class."

Tearing her gaze away from him wasn't easy, but it was necessary. She hadn't come this far to be sidetracked by an attractive man, with an obvious bulge in his pants. Gazing out to the class centered her once more and she took a deep breath before speaking.

"Next, we'll return to the earlier lecture portion of this class wherein I went over the principles of pleasure. As you know, pleasure will vary depending on the participants. For women, receiving the ultimate pleasure will depend on things like psychological history, sexual history, relationship history, and even her mother's relationship and sexual history."

He moved as she spoke, walking from where he'd originally stood at the door, to the other side of the room. She tried to focus her gaze on two women sitting in the center, but she could see him in her peripheral. She could feel the warmth of his gaze moving over her like an invisible cloak. And he was listening to her, hearing every word she spoke about pleasure and sex. The thought excited and frightened her.

She licked her lips.

"There are also factors that pertain to all of us, man and woman. Things that men will need to be aware of as they set out to pleasure their women and vice versa. The first of all pleasure principles is that it's not simply about the physical. It's about so much more."

He'd moved closer and was now standing to her right now, about fifteen feet away. She should've been alarmed. In the five years since she'd been in the adult entertainment industry, she'd learned to keep her distance from students. A few of her colleagues had endured horrific experiences because they hadn't been careful. But Portia didn't feel fear at Ethan's closeness. She felt anxious.

The unwanted sensations made her move quickly through the rest of the hour-long class and breathe a sigh of relief when the last student thanked her and left the room. But he was still there. She wasn't surprised, throughout the rest of the class she'd felt the heat of his gaze on her, the pressure building between her legs at his proximity and the throbbing of her temples each time she mentally admonished herself for feeling anything where Ethan Henley was involved. Still, she couldn't deny the feeling as if his mind and body were reaching out to hers. Maybe she was the only woman in the world who thought this way. She'd centered her instruction on mind and body. She'd also based her life— since leaving Providence when she was seventeen years old—on trusting her gut. Today, at this moment, her gut said to turn around and face him.

She did and saw quickly that they were now up close and very personal.

"Portia?" he asked, his brow furrowed.

He was everything she remembered and so much more. The scent of his cologne was spicy and woodsy tickling her nostrils until slithers of desire awakened a chorus of butterflies in her stomach. His shoulders were wider than she recalled, like a line-backer. His chest was muscular back when they were in high school, but was now more alluringly defined in the tight black t-shirt he wore. He was still much taller than her five-foot one-inch stature, the line of his jaw was strong. His complexion was a fawn hue, a mixture of his Black father and Caucasian mother. The color of his lightly trimmed beard and low-cut hair, was sandy brown, and the green eyes that were currently bearing down on her were full of brown flecks.

"Hello Ethan," she said, her voice much stronger than she was actually feeling.

"You're back." He stated the obvious.

"I'm working." Why she felt compelled to provide a reason, she wasn't quite sure.

He raised a brow. "Your job is teaching Blow Jobs 101?"

She managed a smile at the incredulous look on his face. It was just like high school all over again. He still thought of her as Plain Portia and she still looked at him like he was the Prince of Providence High and the star running back of the football team.

But that was then. This was now and Portia wasn't that teenage girl anymore.

"I teach people how to find their pleasure," she said, holding his gaze.

"Really?" She hated that his gaze still seemed to question her and was shocked when he touched a finger to her bottom lip. "Can you teach me?"

2

*D*esire shot like an arrow and landed straight at its mark —between her legs. Portia shifted slightly, hoping the pressure her clenched thighs created would staunch the pulsating need that Ethan inspired.

"Private sessions aren't available." She'd tutored Ethan in Algebra when they were in high school. Math had been her favorite subject and even though he was two grades above her, she'd been taking advanced classes while Ethan struggled with the classes on his general curriculum. Without her helping him to pass every quiz in that class, he wouldn't have been allowed to suit up and play most of the games of his senior year and he'd thanked her for that profusely at the time, only to let her down when it really mattered. "And after this conference, I won't be conducting any workshops for the next six months."

He was still touching her. She never allowed anyone to touch her, but this was Ethan. There'd been a time when she'd craved his touch more than living. For three years all she'd wanted was to be Ethan's girl. Now, twelve years after she'd considered herself over that childish crush, his thumb had moved from her lip but still rubbed along the line of her jaw as he watched her intently. Too intently. Almost as if he were in awe that he was actually touching her. Well, that made two of them, but she had no intention of letting him know that. She cleared her throat and arched a brow seconds before he spoke.

"Are you quitting?" he asked with a raised brow.

Why was that so sexy? She was an adult now and she'd seen her fair share of men smiling, smirking, blinking their eyes or licking their lips to get her attention. Ethan had never needed to do any of those things, her teenage heart had been like putty in his hands. Why did he still have this effect on her?

And why was she letting him touch her when she knew he didn't like her. Or he pitied her as most of the older kids had during high school. Plain Portia who wore braces and plain dresses for two years straight. While her parents hadn't been poor in the financial sense, Wayne and Judy Merin didn't mingle with many people in Providence. Her father's job as a lobbyist and her mother's as her father's twenty-four-seven assistant, kept them terribly busy. Sometimes even too busy for their only child.

"I'm not a quitter." Those words had become her mantra over the years, now she said them with a sense of pride. She hadn't stopped tutoring Ethan when Cassidy Lewis approached her in the bathroom and told her she was making a fool of herself gawking over a guy that would never want someone like her. Cassidy had then gone a step further to emphasize what type of girl she'd thought Portia was by tugging on one of the stray strings from Portia's sweater until it made a big hole on her shoulder, an impossible spot to cover for the rest of the day. She'd had a tutoring session with Ethan that afternoon and he'd pretended not to notice the hole, just as he always acted as if he hadn't notice her other worn and dated clothes.

With memories from her past bombarding her, Portia turned her face so that his hand fell away. She took a casual step back from him and then moved to the other side of the table where her props and notes were. "I'm actually on a book tour and I have many stops to make in the coming months. So I won't have time for my usual classes."

She reached under the table and pulled out the bin she used to store her items.

"You wrote a book?" The incredulous tone in his voice was so familiar and she bristled with offense.

Pulling a wet wipe from the container she'd kept in the bin, she began cleaning her props, acting as unaffected as possible. Seconds later she glanced up at him. "Yes, I wrote a book. Is that so hard to believe?"

"No. No, it's not." He shook his head as if to emphasize his denial. "I always knew you were smart."

Everybody knew she was smart. That was one of the biggest reasons the kids tortured her so much. For the life of her, Portia would never understand why children thought being smart was akin to having an incurable disease.

"And talented," he added when she couldn't find the words to respond to him. "You've got a really...ah...enticing talent."

That wasn't the worst a guy had said to her after one of her sessions. Her publicist had suggested the publisher hire a body-guard to travel with her during the tour just in case someone got out of hand or wanted more than the lesson she offered for the entire class. Portia had declined. She could take care of herself. After all, defending herself against a guy who'd thought he could take something from her was exactly how she'd ended up with this career in the first place.

"I'm really good at what I do." While becoming an intimacy instructor was far from her parents' dream of her going into poli-tics, Portia was in no way ashamed of the multi-million-dollar empire she'd built within the sex entertainment industry. In fact, outside of the money she'd earned, shedding the shy awkward smart girl persona she'd been flanked with throughout her child-hood, after that fateful incident her senior year in college, the sex entertainment industry with its uninhibited nature had empow-ered her in ways she'd never imagined.

"I have to agree with you there." He cleared his throat and gave a little chuckle before coming around the table and taking her wrists in his hands.

Why did he keep touching her? And after all that had happened between them, why did she keep letting him?

"I was very...uh, intrigued by your little demonstration," he said.

Portia didn't want to intrigue Ethan Henley. Not anymore. "I have to pack up so I can head back to the hotel."

"I can drive you to your hotel." He offered and stepped even closer.

Ethan could drive her absolutely crazy if she let him! But that's not what Portia was here to do. She was promoting her book and just passing through Alexandria. When the conference was over, she would stop in Providence to put her godmother's house on the market and then she would be moving on. Again. Nowhere in those plans had she anticipated seeing Ethan Henley. "No, thanks. My publisher arranged a car service for me."

"I could follow the car to your hotel and we can have a drink." If this wasn't someone she'd shared many memories with, his offer would be creepy and she'd be doing everything in her power to get the hell away from him, but again, this was Ethan.

His eyes had grown darker, his voice huskier and his thumbs were now circling over her racing pulse. No other guy had ever come close to comparing to Ethan in Portia's mind. Even when she'd gone off to college and had allowed herself to be with other men, somewhere in the back of her mind Ethan still lingered. Now he was here, standing so close and looking as if he wanted to devour her. She could barely breathe with the weight of that thought. The girl that had left Providence when she was seventeen and a half would've thought Ethan was playing a cruel trick on her, much like the one he'd pulled when she was in the tenth grade. The woman and professional that she was now, recognized the look in his eyes, his posture, and the tone of his voice. He was aroused. She'd allow herself to bask in that truth later, but for now, she had to stand her ground.

"Are you suggesting a drink or sex, Ethan?" She was pretty sure he was suggesting the latter and even surer that she wasn't interested. She couldn't be. Not again.

He looked surprised at her words, but that didn't slow his roll at all. Ethan pressed closer to her, so close she could feel his thick erection. That was really all the answer she needed, but of course Ethan had to speak.

"We can have both." The offer of a lifetime, or it had been once upon a time.

By way of her tingling nipples and the dampness she now felt as the thin material of her panties pressed against her throbbing skin, her body screamed, *"Yes! We certainly can!"* But her brain insisted, *"Hell to the no!"*

She swallowed hard a few times and then finally replied, "I don't think so."

Where was this Ethan twelve years ago? When she'd desperately wanted him to ask her to the prom? She would have gladly given him a drink and sex that night. After watching so many of her mother's classic old movies about teenagers in love and their high school romances, she'd longed for hers to become a reality. But Ethan had never turned into the Danny Zuko to her Sandy from *Grease* or the Jake Ryan to her Samantha from *Sixteen Candles*. He'd remained the star of the football team who hung out with other jocks and cheerleaders and barely gave her the time of day.

Sure, he was interested in having sex with her now, but Portia wasn't. She'd left that girl behind a long time ago and no amount of great smelling man with smoldering seductive eyes and a hard-on that made her mouth water, was going to change that.

"I'm not interested." A statement she'd made many times over the past years, but one that validated the self-assured, self-reliant woman she was today.

To further state her claim, she pulled her arms away from his grasp and continued to pack her belongings. She didn't look back at him, just kept moving and packing. The faster she got this done, the sooner she could get away from him.

"How long have you been doing this?" He decided to speak again after standing there for a few moments of silence.

"Five years," she replied and clapped the lid down on the bin. She reached across the table to grab all her note cards. Some were further away than others, so Ethan picked them up and handed them to her.

Portia looked up at him and then down at the cards in his hand wondering what he was thinking about what she'd done with her life. Not that it mattered to her, she just wondered. Taking the cards from him, she included them with the stack she already had. "Why are you here, Ethan?"

Why now? she wanted to ask.

"Work," he replied. "I mean, a friend needed an emergency delivery, so I brought it to him."

"But you still live in Providence?"

He nodded. "I left for a while. Went to D.C. to work. But I've been back in Providence for a little over a year now."

Back where he belonged, she surmised. Because every time Portia had thought of Providence, she'd thought of Ethan. There was no one without the other, which was a big part of the reason she'd never come back.

"Oh," she said and slipped the cards into her bag.

Pulling the strap of the bag onto her shoulder, she bent down to lift the bin, but the top slid off and one of the "King Cock" dildos she'd used for her last demonstration fell to the floor. Cursing, she set the bin down and knelt to pick it up.

"I'm glad you've come back," he said the moment she wrapped her hands around it.

Her fingers trembled as she attempted to look up at him. But what Portia saw instead was the thick bulge pressing against Ethan's thigh. Her fingers clenched the dildo as thoughts of rubbing the bulge in Ethan's pants filtered into her mind. She swallowed again, but it didn't help. Damn her traitorous body.

Ethan knelt down in front of her. He didn't touch the dildo, but he grabbed her wrist and guided it back to the bin until she released it.

"Let's go back to your hotel." It was a sincerely spoken invitation, whispered as he brought her wrist up to his lips to place a soft kiss on the spot where her pulse thumped.

It was the sexiest thing Portia had ever experienced. And in her line of work, that was saying a lot. It was saying so much that her chest heaved with indecision.

Ethan wanted her to say yes.

He hadn't seen her in twelve years and admittedly hadn't thought much about her in that time. It didn't make since why suddenly he felt it was so important that she agree and let him follow her back to her hotel. She was a part of his past. Part of the years when he lived at the Grace House for Boys because his mother walked out on him and his father when Ethan was six years old, and his mean, bitter father had eventually drank himself to death on Ethan's fifteenth birthday.

But he'd remembered her instantly. Well, after he'd gotten over the fact that this woman was standing in front of a room full of people giving a dildo the type of blow job Ethan had only ever dreamed of receiving. The memory of her mouth had come back first. He'd always used to stare at Portia's mouth. She had full lips that weren't too big for her pixie-like face. No, they always seemed to be just the right size by Ethan's estimation. Today they were glossed and her eyes—hazel eyes, he noted as he stood close to her—were brighter than he recalled. Her hair was the same, yet different. Wild and frizzy curls was what Ethan recalled of Portia Merin. Today those curls seemed soft and sexy as they hung past her shoulders and down her back. So many curls in a dark brown and golden hue that accented her caramel complexion.

Her body was also different, in an intoxicatingly delicious type of way. Portia was still a petite woman, but her curves had definitely filled out over the years. She wore what should've been a simple black dress, but the way the material molded over every line and curve of her body was mouthwatering. Her shoes were high heels and even the orange painted toenails were sexy.

Yeah, he wanted to follow her home, like a dog following a bone. A part of him also wanted to know what or who had put that look of trepidation in her eyes.

"That's not a good idea," she was saying as she stood up.

Ethan stood too but didn't back away from her. Sure, he was in her personal space and normally he knew the socially correct distance he should stand from a woman whom he was not sleeping with. He knew what to say and what not to say to women to assure them that he was not some random asshole trying to push up on them, or to make them uncomfortable in any way. His years in the Secret Service had taught him a lot of things like restraint and confidence. Other things, like common sense, he'd learned from living the type of life he had. Yet, he couldn't seem to stay away from Portia.

And she didn't seem to mind. That was also a key point in what was happening between them. She wasn't trying to move away from him, nor was she threatening to kick his ass if he didn't back up. Ethan was encouraged by both facts.

"Why?" he answered when he finally realized that she was responding to his comment about him following her back to her hotel room.

"I don't know——" she started to say and then stopped.

Her tongue slipped out, swiping her lower lip quickly, but in just enough time to send an instant jolt of desire soaring through his body.

"Oh, I think you do." He reached out to touch her chin, just beneath the lip she'd just licked.

Her skin was soft as he took a chance and rubbed the pad of his thumb over her bottom lip again. Her eyes grew darker, the hollow between her neck and her collarbone pulsing as he suspected her heart rate had picked up a notch, just like his. This was insanity. He'd gone to school with Portia and there'd never been this type of arousal between them. Sure, they were just kids back then, but he'd been sexually active back then too, just not with her.

"You obviously know what to do with those items in your bin," he continued. "I'm just offering to be a live candidate for your instruction."

Ethan was offering a whole lot more than that. He wanted inside of her now. The urgency of that admission slammed into his brain, pressing the good sense he'd worked so hard to hold onto aside. He had no idea where Portia Merin had been in all this time, and that wasn't the most important tidbit of information he expected to acquire by going back to her room. Was she married? Or otherwise committed? Those were big points in Ethan's mind, points that should and could never be ignored. Yet, he hadn't asked that question because he was mesmerized by her mouth.

"I know my job," she said before stepping away from him.

She turned so that he had another glimpse of her delectably round ass and his painfully hard dick pulsated once more.

"I remember you and the rest of your crew from Providence High," she continued.

This time, as if to make a point, she snapped the lid tightly onto that bin before lifting it into her arms and perching it on her hip. Now, why the hell was that so sexy? He watched people lift and unpack boxes on a weekly basis at the bar, but never had he felt as if he might shoot his shot in his boxers. This was a ridiculous situation and he should have simply kept walking past the door to this room, regardless of the sounds he'd heard. Yet, here he was. And there she was, standing a couple feet away from him, hair a wild mass of curls around her perfectly pretty face, lips pouty and inviting as hell.

"More importantly, I haven't forgotten what you and your friends did to me behind the bleachers when I was a sophomore and you were a senior. So you can just save your sinful smile and silky voice for the next woman. I'm not interested."

Portia walked straight toward him at that moment, pushing past him with a strength Ethan hadn't expected. He stumbled out of her way and watched her, dumbfounded, as she walked out of the room.

3

*T*here's no place like home.

Portia couldn't help but recite the famous line as she stepped up onto the first of three wide front steps late Monday afternoon. The paint was cracked on each, but she slowly took one after the other until she stood on the porch just a few feet away from the cut-out gray and white screen door. Nostalgia flooded her as she looked to one side where a swing hung, with rusted chains holding it to the roof of the porch.

How many afternoons had she spent laying on that swing, rocking back and forth while she read a book that took her to somewhere far from Providence and the cruelty she'd endured here?

Damn, she hated this place.

With determined steps, Portia crossed the porch and grabbed the handle to pull the screen door open. The handle wobbled and she had to use her other hand to hold it in place while she pulled —gentler—this time. When it finally opened, she stepped closer to the front door, its white paint also peeling in places. But the clear white knob tugged on her heartstrings as another bolt of memories soared through her mind.

They were diamonds. Every doorknob in Sunny's house were jewels and when she was old enough, her dotting godmother would gift them to her and Portia would be rich enough to travel wherever she wanted to in the world. Her ideal destination always included a place far away from Providence.

Shaking her head, she thrust a hand into her bag and shuffled through the things inside until she found the key. It was on a ring designed like a huge sunflower, of course. Gladys "Sunny" Shakur, an eclectic and high-spirited woman, had always loved her flowers. Using the key to unlock the door and push it open, Portia then stepped inside. She'd never imagined she would be standing in this foyer, her Kate Spade ballerina flats on the old planked wood floor again. But the package with instructions and keys had arrived at her apartment in Seattle hours after the surprise call she'd received from Sunny months ago.

"How's my Ladybug?" Sunny asked the moment Portia had answered her cell phone.

"Sunny! Hi!" she'd exclaimed with sincere excitement because it had been months since she'd heard from her godmother.

Just before Christmas, Sunny announced she was flying out on New Year's Day for a missionary assignment in Haiti. Portia had only been partially surprised. Sunny Shakur was not the type of woman to let roots grow under her, at least that's what she always told Portia. The years between Portia's twelfth birthday and her high school graduation, Sunny had planted herself in Providence, contradicting her own mantra for a time.

"I wanted to tell you I'm heading out again, going to Haiti this time. Got some work to do over there."

Sunny was always straight and to the point, a trait that Portia tried to learn in her adult years.

"Okay. Well, when will you be back? My publisher has scheduled a book release tour starting at the end of July, so I was thinking of taking a couple of days to visit with you while I'm on the East Coast," she'd said.

"That's another thing I was calling about. I need you to do me a favor," Sunny told her in the husky voice that was more than comforting to Portia.

As her godmother had been the only family member Portia had that gave her anything resembling compassion throughout her life, Portia had come to love that voice.

"Anything," she'd immediately responded.

And months later, Portia was standing in the foyer of the yellow Victorian on the corner of Langston and Mulberry Streets in Providence, Virginia. Her assignment was to meet with the real estate agent, Cynthia Curtis, and complete all the paperwork to put the house up for sale.

Closing the door behind her, Portia dropped her bag on the antique table and looked around. Everything was the same. From the musky aroma of incense to the eclectic mixture of French Victorian and Afrocentric décor. Sunny was a woman of many different tastes, none of which she ever apologized for or explained. In her words, "I am who I am, and those who don't like it can kiss my entire ass!"

Portia smiled at that thought. Sunny had been her savior on so many occasions, she would do anything for her. Which is why she was in this town where the children had hated her and her parents had disowned her. At least her parents had moved to D.C. a few years ago, so there was no possibility of her running into them here.

Even still, she whispered "Not for long," as she moved through the empty rooms of the house.

The real estate agent would be here at any moment. The signed and notarized Power of Attorney to handle all of Sunny's legal and medical dealings was in her bag and her flight to Charlotte, North Carolina was scheduled for tomorrow morning at nine. Portia would meet with the agent, drive back to the resort in Alexandria, find herself some dinner and prepare for the next stops on her book tour.

The muffled ringing of her phone drew her attention away from the house and its memories and she walked through the arched doorway of the parlor and then the living room to get back to the foyer where her purse was.

"Hello?" she answered after finding the phone.

"Ms. Merin?"

"Yes, this is Portia Merin."

"Great. I'm Cynthia Curtis from the Thurston Realty Company. I know we were scheduled to meet at five this afternoon, but I'm running a little late. I should be there closer to six, if that's alright with you. Or we can reschedule for tomorrow afternoon?"

"No!" Portia snapped and then cleared her throat. "I mean, no that's not possible. I'm flying out tomorrow morning." She looked at her watch and resisted the urge to sigh. "I can wait until six."

"Wonderful! I'm so excited about seeing the house and getting it onto the market. It's a historic home so I'm sure there'll be lots of interest in the property. Sunny didn't let too many people inside when she was here, so we'll definitely schedule an open house to show what a magnificent house it is."

"Right." Portia agreed. "It is a magnificent house."

After disconnecting the call, Portia resigned herself to being here a little while longer. She decided to walk through the entire house while she waited. The moment she stepped upstairs; Portia knew she'd made a mistake. She should have just stayed downstairs.

The room she used to stay in when she was here was exactly the way it had been when she'd last left it. A full-size bed with white iron head and footboards with a pink flowered bedspread sat in the center of the room. The walls were covered in pale pink wallpaper. At the large window were white lace curtains. Portia's bedroom at the ranch style house she'd lived in with her parents, just six blocks away, had a twin-size bed, a desk and a computer.

Wayne Merin was as frugal as they came. No matter how much money he made working for Nivas Associates, a top lobbyist firm, his house had still functioned in a minimalistic manner. His wife, Judy, abided by Wayne's every rule, regardless of how their only child may have suffered. Portia had let them down from the moment she was born a girl. In her parents' mind, her failures continued when she decided to attend Spelman instead of Yale and chose to study psychology and women's studies, instead of political science.

"You can only walk your path, Ladybug." Sunny had told her one of the many nights Portia had spent at her house when she was a junior in high school. "At one time Judy and I were as thick as thieves, signing on to fight the injustices in the world side-by-side. Then she met your daddy and Wayne turned her into a totally different woman. Now's your turn to be the woman you're meant to be. Not what somebody else expects of you."

Those were the words that pushed Portia to apply to Spellman and to rejoice the moment she received the acceptance letter.

To pass the time, Portia moved to the closet where she began going through her old boxes, laughing at some things and crying about others. So many memories and feelings were locked in this room. From the many spiral notebooks she'd used as journals to the magazines she'd read before cutting out pictures of her favorite entertainers. One particular picture still had tape on its back and she held it in her hand remembering the Keyshia Cole song simply titled *Love*, that she'd sung at the top of her lungs almost every time she'd finished a tutoring session with Ethan.

In seconds, her mind was instantly back to those times when

she and Ethan sat all the way in the back of the library. He always pulled his chair close to hers so they could share the thick Algebra textbook he'd carried from school as if he actually understood what was going on in that class. She hadn't been particularly fond of numbers, but once she memorized a formula the rest came pretty simply. The concept of numbers and letters together to create an equation completely baffled Ethan. But he needed to pass the class in order to play and everyone in school wanted him to play. Everyone including her.

"Remember that both sides have exactly the same value," she'd said one afternoon. She wrote the equation on a piece of paper in pencil.

"How do you know all this stuff?" His question had startled her. She'd always had to try hard to remain focused on the work instead of on the way Ethan looked in his football uniform, or how great his smile was when he was at the table goofing off with his friends in the cafeteria. But now he was staring at her instead of at the paper or the textbook.

"I just know." She shrugged and tried not to obsess over the faded jeans she wore that were just a little bit too high, and the long-sleeve shirt with the material thinning at the elbows. She'd worn the shirt because it was royal blue, one of her favorite colors and she'd styled her hair in two braids because her natural curls were unruly.

"I mean, do you study all the time? Is that how you know everything? You're easily the smartest girl in all your classes." When she looked up at him again it was to see him staring at her ear—both her ears were pierced and she wore cubic zirconia studs in them.

It had taken all her restraint not to reach up and touch the earring self-consciously. Did he know it wasn't a real diamond? Did he really expect her to wear diamond earrings? While his clothes were definitely more stylish and fit better than hers, Ethan didn't have a lot of money either, especially not staying at the group home with the rest of his friends.

"I study when I'm supposed to, which is why we're here right now. You've got a quiz tomorrow. I've taken Ms. Holback's Algebra I and II classes, so I know all her tricks. You really have to study the formulas. From there it'll be easy, just addition, subtraction, multiplication and division. All the basic in math."

He shook his head. "Nothing about you is basic."

The comment had taken her so off guard she'd dropped the pencil and sat back in the chair as if she'd been pushed. Ethan had worn a short sleeve t-shirt that day, white and fitted tight across his chest. He lifted weights every day in the gym after school and it showed.

"I'm just me," was all she'd managed to say. It was probably a very weak remark and she knew Cassidy Lewis and the rest of the cheerleaders would've had some practiced coy response instead. They would've flipped their long relaxed and styled hair over a shoulder and giggle and Ethan would stare at them like he'd dreamed of them every night. The thought irritated her, and she shrugged again.

"You're pretty great," he'd said as if it were a simple truth and she needed to believe it.

She hadn't, but she'd also never forgotten that he'd said it.

Not even all these years later as she hummed the song in her mind. The sound of a car passing outside had her turning to look out the window. The sun had set and it would be getting dark soon. Time had really flown by as she'd sat here reminiscing. Glancing at her watch she noted it was now close to eight-thirty. Where the hell was Cynthia Curtis?

If there was one thing Portia hated, it was someone disrespecting her time. She picked up her phone to call the agent but paused when she saw the text message that was left an hour and a half ago. Cynthia wasn't going to make it today. She apologized and assured Portia that they could take care of everything via email if necessary. Irritated that her plan had been changed and undecided as to what to do now, she locked the house and headed for the rental car she'd parked at the curb.

Minutes later, she rode past Main Street and was headed toward the industrial area of town when she passed a bright blue sign that read: Game Changers Bar & Grill. Her stomach growled and she thought about turning around and going into the restaurant to get something to eat. But it was past time for her to leave Providence. As much as the things in her room had made her feel nostalgic, the town still held bad memories. One of which was Ethan, the guy who'd been part of the best of her times here and some of the worst. How ironic that he'd been the first person from this town she saw a few days ago?

Just as her thoughts began to circle back to Ethan and the complicated friendship they'd shared, the car began to swerve and she held tight to the steering wheel to keep from going through the guard rail and down an embankment. There was a loud thumping sound as the vehicle continued to move at a much slower pace, until she finally pressed on the brake to stop. Switching off the ignition, she stepped out of the car. Slamming the door closed, she moved quickly to the front of the car getting out of the way of oncoming traffic whizzing by.

Damn. Damn. Damn!

She almost screamed the words, but instead shook her head as they filtered through her mind. After waiting for the realtor and going through blasts from her past, now she had a flat tire. Her stomach growled again…or was that thunder? She looked up to see that the sky was indeed dark, but not with night. With heavy gray clouds that looked as if they would burst at any moment.

"Please, no. Not now," she prayed as she went back inside the car to grab her cell phone. AAA was one of her speed dial numbers so she pressed the button and continued to pray that someone would come to help her soon. Like, before the sky opened up and rained on her as a welcome home present.

"I'm telling you, it was like nonstop sex all damn night," Rod said after downing his third shot of whiskey.

After the three beers he had while playing darts, and the glass of wine he'd forced himself to drink while trying to score with Meta Haynes, the new fourth grade teacher in town, Rod was slumped over the end of Ethan's heavily glossed dark oak bar top. His blonde hair was tousled and his fingernails were dirty from working at the construction site all day. One more drink and he was cut off. Ethan had already warned Jeret they were going to need black coffee ready to be poured at any minute. Lance would have to drive Rod home since he lived the closest to the apartment building where Rod stayed.

Nobody left Game Changers drunk with car keys in hand. That was a standing rule the guys decided on when they'd dreamt up the plans for the bar and grill.

"They were coming out of this big room horny as hell and looking for action. And we were just sittin' in that room harrassin' Charlie about gettin' tied down," Rod continued, his eyes glazed with inebriation and desire.

Ethan chuckled to himself as he used a cloth to wipe the spots of the bar where nobody sat. Monday nights were pretty slow for them when it wasn't football season. Noah Jordan, the marketing guru for Game Changers, was trying to come up with special events that would bring customers into the bar on a daily basis. The manager, Delano "Del" Greer, thought the idea was too fancy-schmancey, as he'd called it. Men wanted things simple, beer, wings and sports on television. Noah disagreed and brought up a very valid point during their monthly poker game and business meeting. His point was that men *and* women liked sports, beer and wings, but women also liked wine, salads and internet access, which was why it was a good idea to have an entertainment spot with a wide range of offerings for both sexes. Ethan agreed with Noah. After that, the poker game had turned to grumbles, accusations of cheating and more debate about men and women. It was one of the moments that Ethan felt glad to be home.

Six friends that met under less than perfect circumstances—they'd all stayed at the Grace House for Boys for one reason or another at the same time—had grown up, went their separate ways and come back together again. A year ago, Ethan would've never thought that would happen, but it had because as his father used to say, "shit happens". As it had when they were teenagers and ended up at the House together, life altering events in each of their lives once again forced them to change course. Now, Del, his twin brother Delancey "Lance" Greer, Jeret McCoy, Noah Jordan, Rochester "Rock" Patterson and Ethan were back together again. Brothers, as they called each other, had come home promising that this new life was a permanent venture. Game Changers was the place for second chances and to prove a point to the people in Providence who once thought they'd amount to nothing.

"Sounds like one hell of a bachelor party," Del said.

He was sitting a few seats away from Rod at the bar, flipping through an overstuffed spiral notebook. Ethan picked up the empty glass in front of Del and refilled it with Sprite. Del was a former DEA agent and didn't believe in drinking alcoholic beverages while on duty—or working at the bar. He was also a workaholic, which was why at nine at night he was still here going over his notes about the marketing plan Noah had given them last week.

"It was!" Rod exclaimed, his words a little slurred. "Tell 'em, Ethan. He was there, he saw all that action."

At the mention of his name, Ethan slowly set Del's glass on a new red napkin. Del lifted his gaze from his notebook to find Ethan's in question.

"Wait, did I just hear that Ethan got some action?" Jeret, asked as he was bringing the first pot of coffee out from the kitchen.

A former Army Ranger, Jeret was tall, fit and dressed like he was on a ranch in Texas instead of just an hour away from the nation's capital. He set the pot of coffee on the warmer and switched it on.

"I delivered the beer," Ethan said, hoping to head off any further discussion.

Especially since what Rod had just alluded to was an all-out misrepresentation of how Ethan had actually spent his Friday night. And the rest of his weekend for that matter. As much as he'd wanted her to, Portia Merin hadn't joined him in his bed—or hers—that night. And the next morning when he'd hit the gym just after dawn, he'd overworked himself on every machine in the place because he'd been still wishing like hell she had. By this morning, Ethan had told himself he was over it. Sleeping with her might've been nice, but he hadn't, and that wasn't the end of the world.

"You were in a place where all this sex was going on and you didn't partake?" Jeret continued, a grin spreading quickly across his face.

Jeret didn't smile or laugh often, not since returning to Providence, but when he did, it reminded Ethan of old times.

"Nobody was having sex," Ethan said, a little too forcefully. "At least not that I saw. There was some kind of fetish conference going on, so there were a lot of…sexual things there."

Including the girl that used to get teased relentlessly by the kids at school, some of whom, Ethan was ashamed that he'd called friends.

"There was even a woman there teaching people how to give good blow jobs." Rod was determined to tell the whole story. He closed his eyes and made a moaning sound. "I sure wish I could've been in that room to see what tips she was giving."

"Why?" Del's expression was deadpan. "You wanna learn how to give good blow jobs?"

Ethan grinned.

"Not funny, Del." A tinge of irritation marked Rod's drunken tone and he motioned for Ethan to bring him another shot.

"Coffee time," Ethan announced and tossed the towel he'd been using over his shoulder as he poured the cup of coffee.

He heard Rod grumbling while he set the coffee pot back onto the warmer and watched his frowning face as he carried the cup to him. When he set the cup down on the bar top Rod frowned and Ethan smirked. "Enjoy."

The last thing he wanted to hear about was blow jobs or sex classes or anything that circled his thoughts back to seeing Portia after all these years. He walked back to where Jeret was still standing across from Del and dropped the towel he'd been using to clean onto the bar top next to him. "It's quitting time for me."

"Got a curfew?" Del asked without looking up from his notebook again.

Ethan shook his head. "You're full of jokes tonight." Even though Del wasn't usually the jokester. Of the twins, Lance was definitely the more laid back and fun-loving one, while Del was serious morning, noon and night.

"I've been here since eight this morning, doing inventory until eleven when we opened," Ethan told him. "Sunday's and Monday's late shift is for you, Jeret and Lance."

"Who made that schedule?" Jeret grumbled.

"He did," Ethan said pointing a thumb over his shoulder at Del. It was one of the many things Del kept in an orderly fashion and because it worked in his favor at the moment, he wasn't about to complain. "See you two in the a.m." He kept on walking toward the end of the bar closest to the door. There was a hot shower and a cold beer waiting for him at his apartment.

"Early," Del shouted to him. "Noah heard from the PR company about advertising, so we're gonna go over that before we open."

"Yeah, I got the text." Ethan pushed through one of the two glass doors that were the front entrance of the bar.

There was another set of double doors that opened directly to the parking lot, but he rarely left through them. He always parked his truck at the corner out front so he could see it from his station at the bar. They didn't get a lot of car thefts in Providence, but there'd been a couple of occasions when patrons from the bar had too many drinks and got a little rowdy upon leaving.

He climbed into the cab of his midnight blue Expedition and checked his phone. His glided a finger over the screen to check for emails and/or text messages, there were none. Just as he was about to feel a spurt of disappointment he grinned at his own foolishness, he hadn't given Portia his contact info the other night, so how could he be expecting her to reach out to him? That was something else he kicked himself for the last two days. He'd let her walk out of that room without trying to get any contact information from her. A few years ago, that would've been totally unlike Ethan's charming way with women. A few years ago, he hadn't been involved with Stacey either.

Shaking his head, he tried to convince himself that memory had no place in his mind, not anymore. His relationship with Stacey was old news. Just like the friendship he'd had with Portia was. Two women, two missteps in his life he couldn't go back and fix.

Forward movement, that's where his concentration was now. Moving on with his life and letting the past live in the past. With those thoughts, he started the engine and pulled out of his parking spot. It was only a few minutes later before huge drops of rain splattered onto the windshield. He turned on his wipers and his radio. His favorite playlists were already loaded so he only needed to hit a specific number to hear designated tunes. Tonight, it was Drake. He needed the smooth lyrics and pumping beats to keep his mind off pretty women with lush lips.

He'd just turned onto the highway when the thought of lush lips fled from his mind as his headlights zeroed in on a plump ass leaning into the trunk of a car. The rain had already picked up as he slowed the truck and passed the woman, but the moment he noticed the front tire of her car was flat, he stopped. He put the truck in reverse and parked in front of the car so that he could get out and help. Stepping out into the rainy night he tried not to notice the jeans, red t-shirt and Jordan Retro 13 tennis shoes he wore were now getting soaked.

A car jack and lug wrench were on the ground near the front driver's side tire. She knew what she was doing and was probably at this moment searching for the spare tire in the trunk. Stopping at the back of the car, he asked, "Need some help?"

The woman's head came up so quickly, she lost her balance and started to flail backward. The flashlight she was holding sent beams of light shooting through the night sky. He moved fast, clearing the remaining distance until he was closer to her. He wrapped his arm around her waist and pulled her close to keep her from falling. When she turned in his arms and slapped her hands against his shoulders, his gaze caught hers.

Her hair was wet, slacked down to the sides of her face. Long lashes with drops of water on the ends, blinked over lovely amber-colored eyes. Thanks to the bright beam of the flashlight she still held, Ethan could see the flecks of gold in those pretty eyes he would recognize anywhere. He could also feel the heat moving steadily throughout his body as he once again stared at Portia Merin.

"I don't need any help," she said quietly, before licking her lips.

"I do," Ethan whispered. *I need help getting you out of my head.* Of course, he didn't say that to her, he wasn't a total idiot. But it was true. As hard as he'd tried all weekend his thoughts had continually returned to her and now, here she was again. "I mean, I do need to help you. I can't just get in my truck and pull off while you're out here trying to change a tire in the rain."

"I know how to change a tire." He didn't doubt that for one minute. In fact, he was certain Portia knew how to do just about anything.

"Just let me help you and then I'll be on my way. I promise. No strings attached."

"I'd probably be more inclined to believe those last words if your arms weren't so tight around my waist." With that she pressed her palms flat against his chest as if she planned to push him away, but she didn't.

And he couldn't let her go. As odd and probably obsessive as that sounded, it was clear they were being drawn together for some reason. "I didn't want you to fall."

"I'm not falling now."

No. She wasn't. But the way she was looking up at him, the way her body remained pressed against his even though he'd lessened his hold at her former comment, it sent a very conflicting message. Her mouth was saying to leave her alone, not in specific words, but he could easily get that message. Her actions, on the other hand, were telling him something different. "Let's make a deal." An impromptu proposal that he hoped she'd go along with. "You let me help you with this tire and I won't ask to follow you back to your hotel this time."

The corner of her mouth tilted in a smile as she shook her head. "Just like you tried to make a deal that we only study

Algebra for half an hour and then we talk about your football stats the remaining thirty minutes."

The memory of those days sitting in the back of the library, or at the diner studying came back with a rush. Per his recollection conflict and indecision had always been their thing. "I enjoyed talking to you. Much like I apparently enjoy touching you now."

She faltered for the barest second before easing closer and slamming her lips into his. It only took a second of dazed delight before he was moaning with satisfaction as his lips parted and her tongue eased inside.

4

*S*he was kissing Ethan Henley.

After all these years, all those nights she'd lay in her bed with her eyes closed tightly, wishing like hell this would finally happen. It was happening. Sure, rain fell in what seemed like buckets over them, her hair and clothes were soaked and the stupid lug nuts on the tire were too tightly screwed for her to get them off. But she was kissing Ethan Henley! Finally!

His mouth was masterful, just as Portia imagined it would be. His tongue stroking hers as if they were long lost lovers having the reunion of a lifetime. She could get with that explanation. This was a reunion. She was finally in the arms of her high school crush. His hands were on her body, one palm pressing tightly against her butt cheek, the other planted firmly against her back. Her fingers curled into the sleeves of his shirt, grazing his hard biceps.

Where did he come from? Why was he here?

She felt like she'd asked those questions before, but still had no answer. And right now, just at this moment, Portia only wanted to ask for one thing. *More.*

The kiss was hungry and urgent. Ethan held her tightly against him, so that she could feel the muscles of his body and the throbbing of his arousal. It was thick and hard and felt as if it were straining for release. Her breasts felt heavy, tight nipples pressed against the thin material of her bra and the blouse she wore. There was something in the pit of her stomach, a swirling sensation. Or was it yearning? Was it something that had been waiting for this contact and would now react accordingly? Or... was it dread? Was this another trick? Another way to embarrass her?

On instinct, she pulled away from him so quickly her thigh banged against the back bumper of the car and she yelled out.

"Whoa." He took a step toward her.

His arms were outstretched as he reached for her again, but she sidestepped him this time.

"What are you doing here?" She resisted the urge to touch her now swollen lips but could feel them still warm and pulsating from the fevered kiss. "Why do you keep showing up?"

He stopped moving toward her at that moment. His eyes were intense as he glared at her. The red shirt he wore was molded to his body so that every chiseled inch of his chest and abs were visible. He looked like a superhero standing there in the rain with her jacked up car behind him.

"I saw a woman stopped on the side of the road, in the rain. I stopped to help," he said, his voice tight with irritation.

And he'd come to save the day, just like a hero often does. Only Ethan had never been her hero and at this point in her life, she wasn't even looking for one. She shook her head and wisps of wet hair slapped the sides of her face. She took another step back, inhaled deeply and released it slowly, giving herself a few moments to gather her thoughts.

"I already called AAA. A tow truck is on the way and they'll take care of the car." And she could take care of herself. This wasn't high school, and she'd learned to guard her feelings and fight back when necessary. So if this was another joke on Ethan's behalf, she'd be ready.

He looked confused or exasperated, not as if he were conspiring something and she tried to rein in the thoughts of self-preservation that came on instinct now.

"But you were trying to fix it yourself?" he asked.

Portia sighed. "I can change a flat tire," she told him. "But the stupid lug nuts are on too tight and then it started to rain. And why did you kiss me?" The last came out abruptly, she hadn't planned to discuss that kiss with him. Still, after a second of seeing the perplexed look on his face, she was glad she'd asked. Catching Ethan off guard wasn't something she'd seen anyone do before, her shoulders squared at the thought that she'd accomplished it after all these years.

He took another step toward her now and a part of her wanted to retreat. The stronger, new Portia stood her ground. She wasn't sixteen anymore and running was no longer an option.

"Because I wanted to taste your lips," he said, his voice like a smooth melody over the monotonous beat of the rain. "I wanted to kiss you that day under the bleachers, but you were upset and you ran off."

"Wait, what?" His words had been clear, she just didn't understand their meaning. She'd been there that day and had replayed it over and over in her mind a billion times. At no point had it ever appeared Ethan wanted to kiss her. In fact, his actions had dictated the exact opposite.

"You and your friends tried to set me up that day. Melissa Bannon snatched a piece of paper I'd been doodling on in chem class. She told her boyfriend, Patrick Riggs, that I had a crush on you. Then she told me that you liked me too and that you wanted to meet me under the bleachers. So I went, like an idiot. I should've known better," she said, pain and embarrassment still as fresh as if this had taken place yesterday. She tried to will the emotions away and replace them with resolve and courage. Twelve years ago, she hadn't had the nerve to argue with Ethan or his friends, to tell them all they were ignorant scum for tormenting her the way they did. Tonight, she wasn't going to let the opportunity slip away.

"I waited under those bleachers for almost an hour. And when you showed up, I was elated and…hopeful. But then you looked so confused and I heard something. Patrick fell from the top of the bleachers where he'd been waiting with a camera to catch the exact moment that you would tell me how crazy I was forever thinking you were interested in me. I felt like an idiot for being foolish enough to believe that you, of all people, wanted to be alone with me."

She'd almost repeated the nickname they used to call her, but she'd promised herself to never say foolishness aloud. Just as she'd sworn she would never be in a vulnerable position with another man. Not after Ethan and then Bobby.

Ethan ran a hand down his face, his eyes a fierce green now. "I wasn't part of any plan, Portia. And when Patrick insisted I go behind the bleachers to find a surprise, I knew he was up to no good. I didn't know it involved you until I got there."

Well, she would've said that announcement was like rain on her parade, but considering the circumstances, she refrained. It was anticlimactic for sure considering all the time she'd spent hating him for that day after all she'd done to help him. Still, somewhere in the recesses of her mind she wondered if she could even believe him. Why would he lie now? Because he thought he had a shot at having sex with her? Not likely. A kiss was one thing, but sex was something she'd never actually considered.

"It doesn't matter," she said finally and looked back as she heard the sound of another vehicle coming.

It was the tow truck. Thank the heavens!

She tried to walk past Ethan, but he reached out to touch her arm. She didn't yank away, instead she met his gaze when he spoke.

"I'm sorry they did that to you. I'm sorry for all the cruel things they did and said back then. But it wasn't me. I was never involved in any of it," he told her.

He sounded sincere, standing in the rain after he'd kissed her brains out.

"And you never tried to stop it." That had been a simple truth that she figured they'd both have to live with. "But don't worry about it now. It's done."

And it was. She slipped her arm easily out of his light grip and walked back to the front of her car, where she opened the door to grab her purse and phone from the front seat. Without looking back to where she knew he still stood, she walked to where the tow truck had come to a stop, opened the passenger side door and climbed inside. While the tow truck driver hitched the car to the back, she watched through the moving windshield wipers as Ethan came around her car and walked to his truck. He got inside but didn't pull off until the tow truck drove past him.

What was he thinking now? Was he still feeling the residual warmth from their kiss? Or was he remembering that day she'd stood there looking at him as her entire world had been shattered? That's how she'd felt that day under the bleachers and she'd never tutored Ethan again after that. She hadn't cared if he played football again or not, she wasn't going to sit next to him at a table after he'd shown her how he really felt about her. But now, what was she supposed to do with all that she'd learned about that fateful day now?

Nothing.

Just like she'd told him, it was done. That moment and so many others had been defining moments for her. They'd molded her into the woman she was now, so she guessed she should be grateful to some extent. At any rate, she wasn't going to be in Providence much longer. All she had to do was take care of Sunny's house tomorrow and then she would be on her way. What happened twelve years ago didn't matter. Ethan Henley no longer mattered.

Even if she desperately wanted to kiss him again.

"She's an intimacy instructor," Camy Greer said two days later while sitting at the bar eating an order of loaded French fries.

Her brother Lance, who sat one bar stool away from her, stopped practicing the tune he planned to play tonight and propped his guitar on one thigh. "Who's an intimacy instructor?" he asked.

Ethan finished drying a tray of glasses. He put them away and moved to the other end of the bar to greet two customers who'd just come in. He was the bartender on duty at the moment, and most of the time at Game Changers as he was the one who had prior bartending experience from his college days. Lance was his back-up on busy nights and the two nights a week that Ethan came in early during the day. But Lance's true love was his music, so he'd convinced Noah that they needed a stage for live music every once in a while. Noah warmed to the idea and began planning on how to get other musical acts to drop by. Their business was really shaping up and Ethan was glad for that. They'd all been through so much; they needed some good light shed on them.

Ethan decided he might need a little more than good light at the moment. He was irritable. He didn't need his friends to tell him that. He'd been in a mood since Portia walked away from him again. That was the second time that woman had left him standing like an idiot staring after her. He was determined not to give her a third time.

He had a three strikes rule. Shit happened in life, but he didn't have to sit back and let it happen to him over and over again. So there were three strikes in his book—one, he chalked up to fate or a mistake, two was like a slap to the back of his head to get his act together and three…Ethan was certain nobody wanted to know what would happen when he got to the third strike in any situation.

So he was through with Portia Merin. Yes, that kiss they'd shared was hot and only sealed his opinion that getting her in bed would be an explosive experience. And he still thought about her curvy body and masterful mouth from time to time throughout the day. But Ethan had seen something else in her eyes two nights ago on the side of that road. Fear and worry. Who or what was she afraid of or what was she worried would happen? He didn't know and truthfully, he didn't have the time or energy to try and find out. His focus now was Game Changers and building something together with the only real family he'd ever had. That was it. He was just fine with never seeing or hearing the name Portia Merin again.

"And she's doing some work on the Sunnydale so she can sell it. I saw the paperwork at the office and Rod's floating on cloud nine because his company won the bid on the job. He's over there now taking measurements or whatever it is he does," Camy was saying when Ethan made his way back to their end of the bar.

She was supposed to be helping out tonight, waiting tables with Glory Jefferson who was also a part-time college student.

"Wait? Plain Portia owns the Sunnydale house?" Lance asked. "I didn't know that. I thought her parents were those stuck up politicians that finally left town a few years ago."

"Her name is just Portia," Ethan interjected. "Portia Merin. And why are you even talking about her?"

He knew his tone was edgy, but he ignored the quizzical looks being tossed his way by Camy and Lance. Hearing that she was still here in Providence had been a shock that he'd also planned to ignore, but he wasn't going to let what had happened to her years ago get started again. Especially not with his friends.

With one brow raised and his fingers moving absently over the guitar, Lance sat back and looked at Ethan. "Yeah, you're right, her name is Portia Merin. She was two years behind us in high school. Cute face, quiet, a little nerdy."

"Hey," Camy said. "Nerdy is the new sexy."

Camy was on track to graduate at the top of her class at Hampton University. From there she planned to go to law school. Del and Lance were paying her tuition and all of the guys were extremely proud of her. She'd had a rough time after their mother died when she was just thirteen years old. Del and Lance were already living at the House by then because they were too rowdy for Elaine Greer to handle while she was battling breast cancer.

"Never in a million years would I have pictured Pla...I mean, Portia Merin as an intimacy instructor," Lance continued.

Ethan almost said she gave a pretty damn good blow job demonstration and a hell of a great kiss, but he declined. He did move toward the bottles neatly lined across the back ledge of the bar and selected the ones needed to fill the new drink order.

"Anyway, I haven't seen her yet. Have either of you?" Camy asked.

"Nah," Lance replied.

Ethan acted as if he was no longer a part of the conversation.

"Haven't seen who?" Glory asked when she joined the group.

Ethan scooped ice cubes from the freezer and dropped them into a shaker.

"Portia Merin," Camy said while chewing.

"She's an intimacy instructor now," Lance added.

"Wow. I don't remember much about her except that her parents kept her on a tight leash," Glory stated. "Intimacy instructor is just a fancy word for sex teacher, right?"

Ethan poured vodka, green apple schnapps and a little apple juice into the shaker.

"Damn! Portia's teaching folks how to have sex. That's...ah... that's really something," Lance said.

Ethan snapped the top on the shaker and began to shake, as if his life depended on the perfect combination of the liquids inside. He moved his arms fast, creating a loud sound and stared across the bar to the walls on the other side of the restaurant where a dozen TV screens were mounted. Baseball was on a few screens, CNN on others and *42*, the Jackie Robinson movie on a few more.

"Isn't it something, Ethan?" Lance asked in a louder voice.

"Yeah, sex is something, when you can get it," he replied. "When's the last time you got laid, Lance?"

Ethan knew Lance would never answer that question, because he'd taken a vow of celibacy after his girlfriend of eight years ran off with her trainer. Lance's vow was only known to the brothers, so Ethan felt a little low for asking, but he desperately needed them to stop talking about Portia and her occupation. The entire conversation was wreaking hell on his mind, and his body, for that matter. He was damn near jubilant that the counter where he was making the drinks hid the raging hard-on he was now sporting.

"I'm going to take this order down and then I'm heading into the back to finish unpacking today's deliveries. You can take over," Ethan said after a few moments of Lance's complete silence.

Another group came in and Ethan took and filled their drink order while sending their food requests back to the kitchen. It was fifteen minutes later when he finally made it back to the stock room. He walked past the neatly stacked rows of shelves and headed straight to the bathroom.

Ethan cursed as he locked the door and leaned against it. His head fell back, slamming into the wood with a thump, once, twice and then a third time as he closed his eyes and tried to force her from his memory. He shouldn't have been this affected by her. Not after twelve years, and certainly not after all he'd been through. But he was. Dammit! He was totally stimulated by seeing Portia giving that blow job and kissing Portia, holding her in his arms and feeling her breasts pressed against his chest. She'd even moved her hips while they kissed. It was a slight motion, but one Ethan knew was in response to feeling his erection.

"Fuck!"

That was both a scream of rage and what he wanted to do with Portia. He gripped his length that pressed hot and hard against his thigh through his jeans. He would not. Could not. He wasn't a horny teenager anymore and he hadn't jerked off since he was fifteen years old. He hadn't had a wet dream since then either, but this morning had been a pretty close call. What the hell was this woman doing to him? And how soon could he get over it, because this was not going to work. He was *not* going to relieve himself to the memory of her licking a damned dildo!

But he was going to continue thinking about her. He hadn't stopped since seeing her at that hotel. And when he realized she'd thought he'd been in on the plan to embarrass her all those years ago, he hadn't been able to get the memories of their time alone and how strange it'd made him feel back then out of his head.

She was the smartest girl he'd ever known and her eyes were the prettiest he'd ever seen. Sure, girls told him he had pretty eyes all the time. It was one of those things his guidance counselor had said would always attract girls to him. Instead of his brains, which he apparently wasn't using since at the time of that meeting in the eighth grade, he'd been failing all his classes. But Portia never said anything about his eyes. She only talked about Algebra.

"What do you like to do in your spare time?" he'd asked her one day when he'd been walking her home from the library. "I mean, besides tutoring guys like me."

"I don't know any other guys like you and you're the only one I'm tutoring."

He'd gotten her name from a list of possible tutors in the guidance office, so he'd just assumed she had other students. Learning he was her only one was a shock, but made him feel good nonetheless.

"But what else to you like to do? You don't play any sports."

"No. I'm not into sports." She'd been staring ahead, but suddenly looked over at him. "Except football. I like football."

He'd grinned. "I love football."

"I know." She'd smiled at him then and something deep inside his chest had warmed. He'd felt that feeling when he was with her before but hadn't really thought too much about it. On this day, he wondered what it meant. "I also like to read and sing."

He'd already figured she read a lot. She was always carrying stacks of books that didn't look like textbooks. The singing was different. He never would've expected that response. "Are you good at singing?" Of course she was, Portia was good at everything. "Can I hear you sing sometime?"

She shook her head so hard he thought those stud earrings would fall out of the holes in her ears. "Do you sing for your boyfriend?" That question had been a surprise to him and by the look on her face, to Portia as well. He didn't know why he'd asked it, the words had just tumbled free.

"No." She spoke the one word softly.

He'd wanted to ask why but they were across the street from her house by then and she'd hurriedly said bye before running the distance to her front door. For a few minutes he'd stood there just staring at the closed door wondering why no guy had snatched her up. She was a hell of a lot nicer to be around than Melissa or Cassidy and the rest of the cheerleaders. She actually spoke in full unique sentences instead of echoing everything he said and following up with an insane giggle. Of course, she didn't dress like the other girls in their skintight jeans and tops with all their cleavage showing, but he liked her quiet style. And her tops were usually fitting enough that he got a good idea of how nice it would be to touch her pert breasts.

But that was never gonna happen. No way was a girl like Portia Merin ever gonna be interested in a guy like him from the House. She probably had her life all planned out—an Ivy League college, grad school, some high-powered career, money and success. All he had going for him was the hope that he'd at least get a football scholarship to pay his way through college. He didn't come from a good family like Portia, but instead from an abusive father who'd finally done them both a favor and died and the snickers of all the grown-ups in town telling him he'd never amount to anything just like his dad.

Walking away that day he knew there was no use thinking of how pretty Portia's eyes were or how he liked her smile and really wanted to hear her sing. She was too good for a guy like him and they'd both be better off if he never told her he liked her.

Ever.

When the memory faded and his mind was once again focused on the here and now, Ethan sighed heavily. He pulled his hands from his crotch and dragged them down his face, still believing that Portia Merin was too good for the likes of a guy like him.

*P*ortia was on her third trip from the house to the car and back. Because of the delay in meeting Cynthia and then Cynthia's not so subtle suggestions that the house would make a much better profit if some renovations were made first, she and Sunny decided to scrap the plan of having movers come in and pack up the entire house and put everything in storage. Now, Portia was going to do most of the packing. She would ship some things to Sunny and put others in storage. The things she wanted to keep herself, she would ship to her apartment in Seattle.

As for the book tour, she wasn't due to her next stop until next Tuesday which was five days away. Rodney Hankin had just left after assuring her that the updates Sunny had approved would be completed by then. Cynthia had proposed knocking down walls and changing paint colors, but Sunny had been…well, she'd been Sunny telling Cynthia via their conference call, what would and would not be changed. There would be fresh paint in all the rooms, new countertops and appliances in the kitchen, no walls would come down and landscapers could come and attack the overgrown shrubbery in the front and back.

Now, it was almost ten in the evening on Wednesday night and Portia desperately needed dinner and a shower before she could work on the outline for her next book. She carried a heavy bag in one hand and a file folder full of research in another. When she came to the screen door, she attempted to open it with the hand holding the bag. The broken handle moved and when she tried to overcompensate, the bag and her folder dropped to the ground. She cursed as she bent down to pick them up.

"Let me get that for you."

She looked up to see Ethan running up the stairs to the porch and kneeling down in front of her. The wave of déjà vu came quick, making Portia dizzy with a mixture of surprise and expectation. *Why was he here and why did a part of her feel so happy to see him again?*

"I can get it." She hurried to pick up the books and papers that had fallen out of the bag because she didn't want Ethan to see them.

"I'm just trying to help, Portia." She knew that and felt like a jerk for acting like he'd come to pounce on her or harass her in some way.

When she finished stuffing everything into the bag, she stood. "I know. Thanks."

Ethan was standing across from her, looking as calmly sexy as always. Today's jeans were a dark denim-wash but the red t-shirt was familiar from the other night. This time she noticed there were words embroidered in black script over the right pocket of the shirt. They read: Game Changers.

"You work at that restaurant near the interstate exit?" she asked.

He stuffed his hands into the front pockets of his jeans and stood with his legs partially spread. "I *own* the sports bar near the interstate exit."

"Oh," she replied. Ethan owned a sports bar. Of all the things she'd considered he might do in his adult life, that hadn't been one of them.

With raised brows, he asked "Shocked?"

"Yes," she said frankly. "You played football. They were talking about scholarships and possibly the NFL when you graduated."

He was expected to go on to become a great college level wide receiver and then to be a top pick in the NFL draft. Portia had gone to every football game, watching in awe as he moved on the field and when he walked off. There wasn't much she hadn't known about Ethan while they were in high school, and nothing that hadn't intrigued and endeared him to her even more.

He nodded slightly. "I went to college, studied criminal justice, graduated and went on to work for the Secret Service because I wanted to do more than run up and down the field for the rest of my life."

There was a terseness to his tone, but she chose to ignore it. She hadn't invited him here so if he was annoyed by her words or her presence, he could leave. That may have seemed unduly harsh, but she wasn't going to be intimidated anymore.

"You could've been rich." She tightened her grip on the handle of the bag and clamped her lips closed tightly. Money meant different things to different people. She'd known that Ethan lived at the group home because his parents were dead and he had no other family. That was part of the reason she'd thought if anyone deserved a free ride to college and a top NFL pick, it was Ethan.

He shrugged. "I wanted to help people more and for the record, I learned how to invest well, so I'm doing okay."

"Right. I understand. Sure, you are. You own a restaurant. I'd say that was okay." She'd also say she was babbling and that made her feel ridiculous. Portia took a deep breath and released it slowly. "Well, it was great catching up, but I need to get inside. I have some things to do."

That wasn't a lie. She had to finish packing up her room and some other things that Sunny wanted in storage. Her agent had also sent her an email asking her about the first chapters to her second book, so she needed to get started on that. She also wanted to get away from Ethan, again. After spending all her teen years pining for this guy, now she couldn't stand to be in his presence. That wasn't true. It wasn't that she didn't want to be around Ethan. It was more like she didn't know how to be around him.

"Yeah, I heard that you were going to be in town for a while. Fixing this place up so you can sell it," he said.

He was looking around the porch now, to the handle on the screened door that was barely hanging on by a nail and the windows that needed to be reframed.

"I'm pretty handy. Noah and I did a lot of the work on The Lofts so I could help you out with some things. You know, free of charge," he said.

Portia had seen The Lofts yesterday when she was driving around town looking for a UPS or FedEx store. She recalled the space used to be an old textile warehouse.

"Ah, thanks, but that's okay. I've hired a contractor. Hankin and Sons."

"Yeah, that's Rod Hankin and his dad. They do good work. I'm sure they'll take care of the big things, but if you need help with just hauling boxes or stuff like that, I can give you a hand."

She opened her mouth to tell him again that she didn't need the help, but didn't want to sound ungrateful. She also didn't want to appear needy, but she hadn't invited Ethan here. He'd simply showed up on her doorstep. Like, he'd been showing up wherever she was since she'd been back in town. It was both annoying and confusing.

"And I also wanted to apologize to you, again."

She sighed because the very last thing she wanted was another apology from him. After his admission that he wasn't part of the plot that long-ago night, she'd forced herself not to think about it or him anymore. "You don't owe me an apology, Ethan. Not another one at least."

Pulling his hands out of his pockets, Ethan stepped forward and she forced herself not to move. It was silly, she instructed people on how to be intimate, how to have orgasms and more, she could certainly stand in front of this man without giving in to teenage panic or adult arousal—whichever one was trying to take over at the moment.

He lifted two fingers to touch her lips lightly. "My friends were wrong. All of us, as kids, were wrong for the things that were said about you and the way you were treated. I can't take that memory or the pain away from you, but I'd like to say that I'm sorry for any part that I may have inadvertently played in the abuse."

Ethan had never called her a name, not that she'd heard. And he was never mean to her, which was a big part of the reason why she'd fallen so fast and hard in love with him. But that was then. She had to live in the now.

"I'm fine, Ethan," she said and moved to the screen door. "No need for any more apologies. And thanks for the offer of help. I appreciate it. But I really need to go."

This time, she grabbed the side of the screen door to open it and was ready to step inside when she turned back to see Ethan still standing on the porch. For a moment she thought he looked confused, but that thought was squashed as he put a hand on the door above hers. He pulled the door open further so that it slipped out of her hand. She didn't move but tilted her head a little so she could hold his gaze.

"That's all I came here for tonight, Portia. I'm not looking for another kiss." But his lips certainly were kissable, and the earthy scent of his cologne was tickling her senses easing her from annoyance to arousal in seconds.

"Neither am I." She lied.

"But you will," he told her.

His gaze dropped to her mouth before slowly easing back up to her eyes.

"You'll ask and I'll oblige because I know you feel what's brewing between us."

Portia disagreed, or at least she planned to deny for as long as possible. "There's nothing happen—" she started to say.

He smirked, a gorgeous lifting of both sides of his mouth and quirking of his brows.

"Right," he said condescendingly. "There's nothing happening…tonight."

Her response was a smirk of her own because bravado was something she'd mastered long ago. Another thing she was exceptionally good at was pleasuring herself. He was trying to put the ball in her court, make it seem like she was going to ask him for more. Well, he had no idea. She didn't need Ethan to assuage the arousal he'd stoked in her. She wondered if he could say the same.

"You go on inside and take care of those "things" you need to do. I'll head home now, but I'm sure we'll be bumping into each other again soon."

She sincerely hoped not. Because while Ethan talked about something brewing between them, Portia desperately needed to push that thought from her mind. While events beyond her control had landed her in the arena of teaching other people how to be intimate and that career had ultimately made her a millionaire, learning how to let go of her own doubts and insecurities was something she'd never been able to overcome.

"Goodnight, Ethan," she whispered.

"Goodnight, Portia," he replied and waited until she'd stepped into the house and closed the door.

Once it was locked behind her, Portia raced up the stairs and closed herself in her old bedroom. She dropped the bag on the floor and immediately flipped open her suitcase to find her personal vibrator. Bringing herself to release was nothing new, and now that she had a visual and the memory of Ethan's lips and hands on her, she would hopefully be able to find a deeper level of pleasure on her own. If she couldn't have the real thing, she could at least have this.

Ethan sat in his truck and stared down at the book he was now holding.

The Principles of Pleasure by Portia Merin

It had fallen under the rocker on the porch when she'd dropped her things. While she'd hurried to pick up each piece of paper and book, she'd forgotten this one. And now Ethan had it.

He rubbed his fingers over the soft matte cover. It was black and white with the silhouette of a seemingly naked couple, legs and arms entwined, the title written in white script letters and her name in bold red print. That night at the resort she'd said she was promoting her book, but Ethan had been too intent on staring at her mouth to pay much attention. Camy said she was an intimacy instructor. Portia was an author and a sex coach. And he was an idiot. Five years with the Secret Service and he was being less than diligent about finding out who the woman who'd been lingering in his mind the last few days really was. A woman whom he should be steering clear of if he knew what was good for him.

As far as he'd known, Portia hadn't been into sex when they were teenagers, she hadn't even had a boyfriend. The woman he'd seen at that hotel definitely knew how to please a man, but when he'd looked into her eyes, when he'd held her in his arms there'd been something else there, something that had nothing to do with pleasure. It was a bit of uncertainty and reservation. He'd thought it was fear initially, but after seeing her again today, he was convinced Portia wasn't afraid of anything. So how did this sex expert, a renowned kinky sex goddess according to the quotes on the back cover of the book, still manage to tremble at his touch? Practice? Faking it? *Who the hell was the real Portia Merin?*

When he realized he was still sitting in front of her house, Ethan started the engine and pulled away. He'd tossed the book onto the passenger seat but couldn't help glancing at it every time he stopped at a red light. He also couldn't avoid thinking about what it might say.

Pulling into the parking lot beside The Lofts, he put his truck in park and again stared at that book. His phone vibrated from his pocket and he pulled it out to stare at the screen.

Meeting tomorrow morning at eight.

Del loved meetings. He took his job as manager of the bar very seriously and thus treated it like a course in college instead of the fun business venture they'd proposed. They were hosting a fraternity party on Friday night, which is probably what the meeting was about. Ethan would have to make sure the staff was well versed in the underage drinking laws in Providence. City council members had squawked about them agreeing to host a frat party at a bar, but Ethan and the guys figured it made more sense to let the group of young men into the bar to have their get together—where the staff could strictly monitor any underage drinking—than to let them have the party at the frat house where liquor could be brought in easily without any supervision. Each of the guys remembered well what it was like to be young with the urge to do any and everything adults told them not to do.

That should've been enough to take his mind off Portia, but it wasn't. He grabbed the book and climbed out of the truck. He entered through the side door with the key card that was only assigned to leaseholders and made his way to the steps. His unit was on the second floor at the far end of the hall, as far away from the other six tenants living in the building as possible. Noah was a former Hollywood stuntman. He'd inherited this building from his grandfather who'd won it in a poker game. The building stood vacant until Noah's return to town a little over a year ago. He hadn't wanted to sell, so Ethan suggested he turn it into loft apartments and make a profit. In exchange for the idea and his help in renovating the place, Ethan became the first leaseholder. Noah had a unit on the first floor near the management office.

Ethan entered his home, locked the door, grabbed a beer from the refrigerator and went to his room. He set the beer on his nightstand and switched on the lamp. Then, he sat on the bed and held that book in his hands. He wasn't going to read a book. Not that he hadn't in the past, but it wasn't one of his preferred hobbies. The Yankees and the Orioles were playing tonight, and he'd bet Lance on the winner. He also had some supply order slips to input into the accounting system Rock insisted they all learn how to navigate. He could take a shower and fix something to eat. The club sandwich he'd had a few hours ago at the bar wasn't enough to hold his appetite. Or he could watch a movie, possibly something on Netflix.

Ethan didn't have to read this book.

But he did.

He took off his shoes and lay back on his bed, reading page after page, until his curiosity and the arousal churning inside him forced him to reach for his phone. He'd gotten her number from a friend he used to work with and no it wasn't ethical. But Ethan was no longer bound by the sacred oath taken upon admission to the Secret Service, nor did he give a damn about the lack of ethics of anyone in that organization. Not after what happened a year ago.

He dialed Portia's number and waited for her to answer. The moment she did, he spoke because Ethan could no longer hold back his questions.

"Chapter 5, Part 1 reads: What you say is just as important as what you do. Is that correct, Portia?" he asked and waiting anxiously for her response.

"Ethan?"

"Yeah," he replied. "You missed one of your books on the porch. I've been reading it and I have questions. In the back there's an email address and a post office box for questions to be sent, but I figured I'd just call."

"How'd you get my number?" She didn't sound as irritated as he figured she could've, so that was a good sign.

He thought about lying, but then figured what was the point? Lies always led to trouble anyway.

"One of my former colleagues in D.C. helped me out on that front," he replied.

She didn't respond.

"I apologize if you feel that's intrusive and mostly out of line," he continued. "You're probably right if that's what you're thinking. But I wanted a way to communicate with you. I wasn't sure I'd actually use it, until now."

She still didn't speak.

He could hear her breathing. She was trying to remain neutral, professional maybe. Probably preparing to tell him it was just a book and not to call her again. Damn, he prayed he was wrong about the latter. More than anything, he wanted an answer from her. A real, satisfying answer.

"Yes," she replied finally, her voice a breathy whisper that made his dick sit up and take notice.

"So we could talk on this phone and it would draw us closer to one another. It would make us feel as if we were long lost lovers, coming back together again."

She cleared her throat. "Words have power. That's the meaning of Chapter 5. In the instance of intimacy, they have the power to break down mental and sometimes physical barriers between a couple. They also have the power to provide each participant with the steps necessary to find their mutual pleasure."

Her voice sounded so husky and sexy, he almost groaned. Words had power alright. Everything she'd just said was in her book. They were words that she'd typed and an editor had read and approved. Yet they were also making his body heat, his muscles tense and yes, his dick grow harder.

"So what I say from this point on could lead us both to pleasure?"

She didn't immediately respond.

"When I kissed you the other night, I couldn't help but think of how sweet your lips tasted," he told her. "Are your other lips as sweet? If I suck on them, will you come in my mouth?"

Her breathing was audibly faster and so was his. His dick was so hard now it pressed painfully against the zipper of his pants. Not even wanting to relive that pain he'd experienced at the hotel; he yanked the zipper down. Reaching into the slit of his boxers, he freed his aching dick, wrapping his fingers around its girth.

"Answer me, Portia. I want to hear your powerful words. Tell me how I can find my pleasure."

His voice had grown deeper, huskier and seemed loud in the solace of his dimly lit bedroom. Was he really on this phone talking sex to this woman he hadn't seen since they were teenagers? And what exactly did he expect her to do? Answer him? Have phone sex with him? He probably needed a good stiff drink instead of a stiff dick in his hands and a hot woman on the other end of this phone.

He'd begun stroking his cock, starting at the base and moving slowly upward until his thumb and finger ran over the sensitive head. She was still breathing heavily and Ethan needed to hear her voice as much as he needed to release the climax that had been building since he'd watched her giving that blow job demonstration.

"I'm wet," she replied in the barest of whispers.

If he'd blinked, he may not have heard her, but he had, and he figured it would take less than sixty seconds and a few more words from her to have him making a mess in his hand.

6

"*J*'m wet and I ache at the thought of your mouth on me there," Portia said and then clapped a hand over her mouth.

What the hell was she doing? She had no idea where the words had come from but recognized them for truth.

She was sitting in the center of the bed in her childhood bedroom, legs crossed with a magazine spread out in front of her. After Ethan left a while ago, she hadn't been in the mood to clean. Her mind—and body—had been too wound up from seeing him again. So instead, she'd taken a shower with her trusty vibrator and afterwards—feeling mildly relaxed—fixed a half sandwich and grabbed a can of soda. The television was on, but she was paying no attention to whatever show that was playing.

When her phone rang, she'd picked it up and answered even though she hadn't recognized the number, but because of the Virginia area code, thought it could've been the construction foreman or someone from the realtor's office. Never in a million years would she have guessed it could be Ethan.

"Yes," he insisted on a gruff sigh. "I want you nice and wet.

Tell me more about being inside of you," he said, his voice a deep timbre that made her feel as if he were lying right here next to her. "How does it make you feel? 'Cause damn, I already know how it's making me feel."

It was making her nervous. This entire conversation, the fact that he obviously had a copy of her book *and* was reading it, and was now initiating phone sex with her, all made Portia jittery as hell. On the one hand, her fingers gripped the phone tightly. On the other, they shook slowly as she forced herself to pull her hand away from her mouth.

"What are you doing?" She had to concentrate to keep a slow and deliberate tone.

That's how it worked for her. Whenever she felt overwhelmed or as if she might be losing control, it took a concerted effort to bring herself back to normalcy—or at least her level of normal. She hadn't felt like this in a while, so she had to tick off every action in her mind to be sure she was gaining the balance she needed. It wasn't easy being Portia Merin.

He sounded as if he were taking a deep breath and then releasing it slowly and loudly.

"I'm reading this book that you wrote and trying not to come in my hand as I match the sound of your voice with the words on the page," he told her.

A vision of Ethan laying on a bed, hard dick in his hand, jerking off to her book...and her voice, sent a quick bolt of lust through her system. It landed like a bullseye between her legs, where her pussy now pulsated.

"They're just words," she said after licking her very dry lips.

"Words that have power," he continued.

He was correct. They could continue to say words that related to a passionate sexual experience and each of them would continue to grow aroused. Or, for Ethan, he could most likely go without the words. In a research paper she'd read while writing her book, Portia learned that male desire could be considered a "solitary affair". Meaning that, Ethan's single-minded pursuit of sexual arousal could exist independent of a relationship. So she could hang up this phone and Ethan would most likely continue with his train of sexual thoughts and masturbate until he achieved orgasm. That's how the male body worked.

The female body on the other hand, or rather, Portia's body, was a different story entirely. There had been no words in research papers or textbooks to describe the type of sex life she'd adopted over the years. The one where she didn't really need words. Or a partner. When she felt edgy or in need of release, Portia found that release alone. She had a variety of vibrators, dildos, and massage tools to help achieve a satisfying outcome. No words, no videos, and no man.

While circumstances beyond her control precipitated her personal sexual situation, confidence and courage had propelled her success in the very field that made her so nervous she now felt a little nauseous.

"Portia? Are you still there?"

"Yes!" she replied overenthusiastically. "I'm here. But Ethan I should tell you that you're just reading a book. It's designed to help coach men and women through finding intimacy with each other. It's not an ah...not meant to, I mean, it's not supposed to..."

"Just tell me how you feel," he interrupted her. "I want to hear you say how you feel when I tell you how hard I am from thinking about kissing you."

That pulsating started again between her legs, building intensely until Portia used her free hand to press a fist there. She had to uncurl her legs and squeeze her thighs tightly for the sensations to subside.

"I don't...I mean, I can't," she began but didn't quite know how to explain her predicament. Or if she even should. This was really none of Ethan's business. It was no one's business for that matter.

"When I watched your demonstration at the hotel, I wanted your mouth on my dick just like that. You had me so aroused I couldn't wait to get you alone so I could ask if I could be your next test subject. And then I kissed you...now I want you, Portia."

He sounded so good. His tone, his words were everything she'd imagined hearing so long ago. Well, maybe not since she was just a teenager then and had zero experience with blow jobs or sexual arousal. But a part of her mind was screaming *"Yes!"* while the other part feared this was the first step to a colossal mistake.

"I just wrote a book, Ethan. I did lots of research and I took psychology classes and I pretend." She made the admission quickly. "I pretend I know what I'm doing. I act out everything that I write, but I don't know. I don't know how to do what you want me to do."

There, she'd said it. She was a complete fake. She could demonstrate sexual acts that she'd never experienced on a personal level and she could write about the origins of intimacy and sexual relations. But Portia had been involved in only one relationship that had lasted six months. She'd had sex with two men in the entire twenty-nine years of her life. And courageous or not, she couldn't participate in a bout of hot steamy phone sex with a guy like Ethan Henley!

Her temples throbbed as her cheeks flushed with embarrassment. She wanted to disconnect the call immediately and bury her face under a pillow. But she continued to take slow, steady breaths and hold the phone too tightly against her ear.

Ethan was quiet for a few seconds before he said, "Where are you right now?"

Portia blinked and looked around the room as if she thought

he could somehow see her. She knew that wasn't possible, so she relaxed enough to answer him.

"I'm sitting on my bed."

"What are you wearing?"

"A Mariners nightshirt," she replied.

"Seattle Mariners, okay, they're not too bad," he told her with a light chuckle. "What are you wearing underneath the night shirt?"

"Ethan?"

"Just questions and answers, Portia. No powerful words and no need for you to pretend," he told her.

Just questions and answers. She could do that.

"Panties. Blue with white polka dots," she replied.

"Cute." He sounded pleased.

She smiled.

"Take them off."

Her smiled disappeared. That wasn't a question.

"I'm here in my bedroom too," he continued. "And I'm taking off my jeans and my boxers. Now, it's your turn."

She couldn't.

But why? He was correct again, he was in his bedroom, wherever that was. And she was here. Alone. Clutching the phone between her ear and her shoulder, Portia slipped her panties down her legs.

"I did it," she announced quietly but proudly.

"Good." She felt like she'd earned a pet on the head.

"Now lay back on the pillows. Spread your legs and touch yourself. You've done that before haven't you, Portia?"

He had no idea how many times she'd done that. She eased back against the pillows slowly, closing her eyes as she spread her legs.

"You've experimented with everything you wrote in this

book." His voice was twenty percent soothing and eighty percent arousing as hell.

Her eyes shot open, her gaze fixing on the popcorn-paint ceiling. "No! I mean, I don't have a—" she paused and cleared her throat. "I don't have a boyfriend and I haven't been involved in any affairs."

"I don't have a girlfriend anymore," he told her. "In fact, I made a resolution to steer clear of any emotional entanglements for a while. But when I need to, I can bring my own release."

She could too. She'd just done so about thirty minutes ago. But again, this was none of Ethan's business. *Why was she even talking to him, or doing what he said?* Because this was Ethan. The only man to ever hold her heart.

Portia let her eyes close once more as she forced herself to relax.

"I know how to bring my own release," she said and was shocked at how sexy she felt just admitting that to him.

"So touch yourself." The directive came instantly. "Touch yourself and tell me how you feel."

While a part of her mind still screamed in warning, her free hand was already moving between her legs. Her skin tingled as her fingers glided over the sensitive skin of her inner thigh. When she touched the warm, plump folds of her vulva, she sucked in a breath. It felt different this time. In the shower earlier, warm water streaming down over her skin, she'd felt a familiar burst of need as she'd moved her fingers and the vibrator through her moist folds. Now, sharp streaks of desire shot up through to her stomach and down her legs. She gasped and swallowed hard at the sensations.

"Ahhh yeah," Ethan murmured. "It feels that good doesn't it? Soft and wet, I'll bet."

"Yes," she whispered. "Soft and wet." That's exactly how it felt, and erotic as fuck.

"I'm hard and hot," he told her. "Press two fingers inside."

Ethan was hard. He was talking to her on the phone and had been reading her book. So he was hard because of her. *Exhilarating.* That was the best word to describe what that meant to her. She eagerly pressed her fingers into her opening. More warmth as tightness gripped her.

"You feel good," she whispered, not sure where the words had come from, but deciding to go with the flow.

He moaned. "You do too."

"Deeper," he insisted.

"Yes," she replied.

"More."

"Mmmm hmmm," she managed, her hips lifting off the bed to meet the thrust of her fingers.

"More, Portia. I want more of you."

His voice was different now, ragged and husky. His breath was coming quicker, almost as fast as her own. She wondered if he were jerking his dick to the same rhythm that she was moving her fingers in and out of her pussy. She wondered and she hoped. And in her mind, he was. She could see it as if he were right in front of her. Ethan was jerking his rigid length. Pre-cum beaded at his slit. She pumped faster, deeper. She moaned, licked her lips and moaned again.

On the other end of the phone, he moaned too and whispered, "More. Yes. More."

His voice was so sexy. The sounds he was making so primal. This was so good. Better than she'd ever experienced on her own before. And then she erupted. Heat soared through her body, her legs began to shake, a tight tingling sensation pooled at her center and hot moisture coated her fingers. The moan that escaped her was long and slow, her eyes closed tightly. Vaguely, somewhere within the pleasure-filled abyss where she'd drifted to, Ethan made a guttural sound and then hissed as if he was trying like hell not to yell out with pleasure.

Silence filled the room seconds later, the phone line, everywhere and embarrassment bubbled up inside her. She moved her fingers over the phone and was about to disconnect without saying a word, but then she heard him.

"That was great, Portia. Your words were so powerful I came harder than I ever have before."

What was she supposed to say to that?

Oh come on! She'd written a seventy-two-thousand-word sex manual, had starred in over fifty tutorial videos and lectured all across the world on this subject. Yet, she couldn't think of one coherent thing to say when the guy of her dreams admitted she'd pleasured him.

"Thank you." She finally managed. "Thank you, Ethan."

She disconnected the call and lay on her bed for the duration of the night wondering what the hell she'd done, and why she hadn't done it sooner.

7

*E*than counted without stopping.

There were forty different beers stocked behind the bar in the Sky Box Lounge. This was Game Changers' upper level where a cigar bar and lounge seating were available for group reservations or special events only. Black leather low-back couches and red ottomans provided seating for up to thirty guests in the rectangular shaped center area of the floor. While on one end a full-service bar allowed for an additional dozen guests. The other side of the room had been transformed to resemble a 1920's speakeasy with its silver tin ceiling and black leather harlequin-patterned club chairs. Rock was a former wrestler who'd picked up the cigar habit while he was on the professional circuit. It had been his idea to add this section and so he made sure to keep only the best cigars, humidors and other paraphernalia for the pastime in stock.

Tonight, was the frat party and a group of twenty-seven guys would be here within the hour to celebrate the upcoming fall semester. There really didn't need to be a reason to have a party, Ethan recalled from his college years. Still, all hands were on deck to make sure the party went off without a hitch and that the customers still visiting the lower level restaurant and bar weren't inconvenienced in any way.

He'd been at the bar since early this afternoon, eight hours and counting. That wasn't normally a big deal. All of the guys spent an insane amount of time working there. This was a new business venture, their livelihood and their lifeline. Except for Ethan, tonight felt like a graveyard shift that he'd never surface from. He'd been moving around methodically, doing whatever needed to be done. Checking inventory, stacking menus on both levels, talking to customers, bussing tables, working the bar, any and everything, he'd done it today. His body felt tight, a headache threatened to break through, and it had been two days since he'd seen or heard from Portia.

The morning after their night on the phone, he'd sent her a text message. Just a simple "good morning", but she hadn't responded. He'd forced himself not to send another message. He didn't beg, nor did he chase a woman who didn't want to be bothered. Especially not a woman that he was sure had more issues than he did. That was absolutely the last thing Ethan needed to deal with. He had his own weight on his shoulders, no need adding more. But he couldn't forget what they'd shared that night, nor could he dismiss the truthful words he'd said to her before she'd gotten off the phone. That had been the best orgasm he'd ever had, with or without penetration. And thinking about it that way was making him cranky as hell.

"Let's do a quick rundown for the night before things get crazy around here," Del said as he walked toward the bar.

Ethan had been standing with his back to the stairway that led up from the front entrance. There was a hostess station at the bottom of the stairs and a smaller one at the top. When he turned it was to see that the gang was all here. Del and Noah took seats at the bar, while Jeret, Lance and Rock stood behind them.

"Make this quick, Del, I gotta get back in the kitchen. Those culinary school kids get delusions of grandeur whenever I leave them alone," Jeret said.

Jeret ran his kitchen like the Army Sergeant he'd been before volunteering for the Ranger program. He inspected the supplies, the food and the uniform of every worker entering his kitchen at least three times a day.

"Think they can cook a hamburger better than you can, huh, Chef McCoy?" Rock asked with a grin.

"Kiss my ass, Einstein," Jeret quipped.

Jeret had always called Rock Einstein because between the six of them, Rock had always been the smartest. Especially when it came to numbers, which is why Rock was in charge of the books at Game Changers.

"Come on, we all know Mal Penning and the rest of his City Council ball busters are going to be watching us like hawks tonight. He and his wife already have a table right by the entrance downstairs so they can see and try to hear what's going on up here," Del said seriously.

Del and Mal had a history. It was a dark and sometimes dangerous history stemming from the time Del broke Mal's nose when they were sixteen and culminating with the reason Del resigned from the DEA. The fact that Mal was now in a position of authority over him wasn't sitting well with Del. But as always, he was trying to handle the situation as diplomatically as possible.

"He's right," Ethan said, trying to give his friend a hand with this meeting. "We have to stay on point tonight. No bullshit. The town's watching and waiting for us to mess up."

Noah nodded. "They've been waiting since we all left the House."

"Because a leopard can't change its spots," Lance added. "Remind me again why we wanted to come back here?"

"Because it's our home," Del said. "We belong here just as much as Mal and his family."

He was right. But Ethan knew what Lance was feeling too. From the time each of them had landed in the House, the good citizens of Providence had written them off as delinquent failures. That's why they put them all in the same house when their situations had been drastically different. Nobody wanted to take the time or the energy to figure out what each of them needed to succeed. They just knew that something had happened with each of them, something they deemed so bad and unforgiving that they needed to be shunned by the good society folk of this small town.

It was all bullshit then and it still was now, which is what fueled Ethan to work so damn hard to prove them wrong.

"Maxie is the hostess up here tonight and Joy will be downstairs," Del continued. He stared down at his clipboard as if the words there would somehow erase the anger, resentment and hurt they all felt at the hands of the good citizens of Providence.

"I'm going to be up here helping Mickey at the cigar bar," Rock said.

Del nodded.

"I'm good at the bar alone," Ethan told him. "But two servers on the floor would be good."

"Right," Del said as he scribbled notes. "I'll send Glory and Kasey up here."

Ethan agreed. They were both experienced and dealt well with all types of customers.

"I'll manage the bar downstairs," Lance said. "Camy's agreed to help out tonight. She's on her way in and we've got four more on staff down there."

"I've got two-line cooks and four preppers in the kitchen," Jeret added.

"I can work the floor," Noah stated. "Make sure everybody has everything they need and nobody drops any balls."

Del nodded. "You take the floor up here and I'll work downstairs."

"Cool." Noah nodded.

"We've got this," Ethan said. "And fuck anybody who thinks differently."

Del's head shot up at his words.

Lance stood with his feet spread apart, arms folded over his chest. "I concur."

Ethan turned back to counting his bottles and checking the rest of his stock before the meeting was convened. He just figured everyone would move on to their assignments. He should've known better.

"You okay?" Noah asked.

Ethan looked over his shoulder to see that Noah and Lance were still standing at the bar.

"Yeah. I'm good. You?" he asked.

"You've been a little short the past couple of days," Noah said.

"No. I haven't."

"Yeah," Lance said with a nod. "You have. Not with customers, because you're always good with them. But in general and with us, you're different."

Ethan sighed. "Is this about the other day? Look, I shouldn't have said anything about your vow of celibacy in mixed company, but you were asking for a comeback."

"Why? Because I was talking about Portia Merin?" Lance tried to look confused even though he knew damn well what he was doing.

"No," Ethan replied tightly. "Because you were being an ass."

Lance nodded and tossed a knowing look over to Noah. "Told ya," he said.

Noah nodded in return. "Yes, you did," he answered.

"What the hell are you two talking about?" Ethan began counting the glasses lined in neat rows on a tray.

"You always were a little touchy about Plain Portia," Noah said.

Ethan sent him a heated glare and opened his mouth to speak. But Noah held up both hands as if in surrender. "I know. I know. Her name is Portia. You used to do that when we were in school too."

Ethan could see where this was going and knew he wasn't going to like it.

"You've seen her since she's been back?" Noah asked.

Ethan didn't respond.

"Rod said he saw your truck heading down the street toward the Sunnydale house two nights ago when he was leaving," Lance told him.

"All roads in Providence lead to home," Ethan said flippantly.

Lance grinned and shrugged. "Hey man, if you finally want to act on that little thing you had for her when we were in school, go right ahead. I ain't mad 'atcha. I saw her at the post office yesterday and she's looking pretty good."

Ethan stopped counting the glasses, but he didn't look up at Lance. He didn't need to. Again, Lance knew exactly what he was doing.

"There was never anything between me and Portia. She was a sophomore and we were seniors," Ethan said. But even to his own ears the words sounded shallow. The only reason there'd been nothing between him and Portia back in high school was the fact that he'd been with one cheerleader after another, or some other senior or even the girl from the community college that had shown up at one of his games. Ethan hadn't made a move toward Portia, even though he'd always felt drawn to her in some way, because he'd been too busy with everything and everyone else.

What nobody else knew was that he'd decided that was the best route to take.

He wasn't sure if that had been a mistake back then, or if it was now coming back to haunt him because since she'd returned, he hadn't been able to keep her out of his head.

"Look, you know we don't pry. We each do what we do," Noah said. "But if you need to talk or release some stress, we can always burn off the extra energy with a basketball game."

"Or poker," Lance added. "I can use some extra cash and you two can't play worth squat."

"I'm good." Ethan looked pointedly at them. "You both know I'm not in the market for a third strike. So I'm good doing what I do."

They both sobered at that look. One of the first things they'd done when they all came back together was tell what had happened to make each of them walk away from the careers they'd thought would last forever. So they knew his story. They knew about his ex-fiancé and the hot blade she'd stuck so callously through his heart.

Lance stared meaningfully at Ethan for a moment and then gave a curt nod. "Stay good, bro."

Ethan nodded in return. "I plan to."

Noah looked as if he wanted to say something else but changed his mind. "Let's get to work. Holla if you need anything," he told Ethan.

Ethan knew that Noah was talking about more than work and the bar when he said that, so he simply replied, "I will."

But he didn't need anything that Noah could help him with. What Ethan needed and what he should probably stay away from were two totally different things. He needed to keep his mind on the bar and making the statement he and his brothers had planned to make in this town. But he wanted, with more urgency than he'd ever experienced in his life, was to be inside of Portia Merin, once and for all.

"Everything is going just fine," Portia lied to her godmother on the phone. "Rod says he's right on schedule to finish everything on Monday. The new HVAC system was installed yesterday. New appliances for the kitchen and fixtures for the bathrooms came this morning. All that's left is the rest of the painting inside and then the outside painting. I'll be on my way to New York late Monday night," she said.

"And your next book signing is Tuesday afternoon," Sunny finished.

"Yes ma'am. I'll still be on track with the book tour."

"How about the new outline and chapters? How's that coming?"

Portia was silent. She didn't want to lie to Sunny any more than she absolutely had to. "It's coming."

"What's the theme of this book?" Sunny asked.

Again, Portia paused. It shouldn't shock her how interested in her career Sunny was. After all, her success was partially due to her godmother's candid advice.

"I'm not sure yet," Portia confessed. "I feel like I've covered all the ground there is to cover in this regard. Sex. The emotion. The physical. Done."

"Oh really?" Sunny asked. "Is that how you think of it now?"

"I'm trying not to think about sex," she said with a sigh. "I'm trying so hard."

Sunny chuckled and Portia stared at the phone quizzically. She shouldn't have said that to her godmother. She should've just kept her mouth shut and got off this call. It was uncanny, but sometimes, it seemed like Sunny could actually read her mind.

And the last thing she wanted right now was for her godmother to know what she was thinking at this moment. What, or rather who, she hadn't been able to stop thinking about in the past couple of days.

"Yes! It's finally happened!" Sunny yelled through the phone.

"What's finally happened? Are you alright?" she asked wondering if Sunny had been paying attention to her at all.

"You've found someone you want to be intimate with," Sunny said. "I knew the day was coming. I told you that patience was a bitch and life was short, so you had to go out there and grab the bull by the horns. Hot damn! You did it!"

Portia shook her head. She had no idea what Sunny was talking about. Her godmother had told her so many things in her years growing up. Some had made sense, others hadn't. Judy, Portia's mother, told Portia on numerous occasions to ignore everything Sunny said. "Her mind's warped from all the marijuana she smoked when we were younger," Judy would say.

But Portia hadn't listened to her mother because between the two former best friends, Sunny had been the one to act more like a loving mother to Portia than Judy ever had.

"I don't understand what you're trying to tell me," she said honestly.

"Yes, you do my Ladybug. You were always good at acting like you had nothing to say, blending into the background so that people rarely knew you were there. But I knew and I watched and now here we are."

Portia rubbed her temple. She had no idea where Sunny's mind was, but Portia knew for certain that her thoughts were once again straying in the direction of Ethan.

"It's a man. My Ladybug has found herself a man."

"No, she hasn't." The denial might've been a little too quick. "I mean, no I haven't!"

Sunny laughed. She had a throaty voice and when she

laughed it sounded more like a rumble of thunder before the explosion of chuckles that could sometimes be infectious.

"For the last ten minutes you've been talking about the house and boxes and your book tour. And I've been listenin' to every word. Especially those you weren't saying."

"Are you smoking again, Sunny?"

"No. And don't start acting like your brainwashed mother. I don't need to be under the influence of any substances to see what I see."

Portia shook her head. "But you're not here to see anything."

"I wish I was, even though it makes no difference because my hearing is just fine. And before you say anything else, I'm just going to leave you with this, take a chance. You went from being sheltered by your idiot parents, to being mistreated by that silly boy in college, and now, being praised for the business you've built. And at no point did you ever stop to think it was possible to love and be loved."

"Sunny, please. You're really going off on a tangent tonight. I'm just trying to keep my promise to you. That's all," Portia said even though there was a tingle of something like doubt or trepidation swirling in the pit of her stomach.

"Go get him," Sunny said. "Get out of that house and go get the man that has you trying like hell not to think about sex."

Before Portia could comment, Sunny hung up. Portia sat on the chair in the kitchen that would be picked up tomorrow by an antique shop she'd called a few days ago and stared at the phone in her hand. She had no idea what Sunny was talking about. There was no man for her to go out and get. No man that was making her think about...Ethan. *How the hell had Sunny known about him?*

Portia pressed the phone to her forehead and closed her eyes. Sunny knew something was going on here the same way she'd known to call Portia nine years ago when she'd been in her senior year at college and had awakened to a total nightmare. As Portia sat on the phone crying to her godmother that day, Sunny had told her to fight back, to take a stand, and so she had. She turned what could've been the most embarrassing moment of her life into a way to both get back at Bobby and make a little money in the process. The surprising success of that one video propelled her to go a step further and start taking business classes. Now, she was the owner and chief content director of Pleasured, Inc., the company which produced intimacy and sexual instruction videos, and an author. She'd made millions in a field that she knew nothing about personally and she was sitting in this kitchen thinking and doing everything except taking the advice her godmother had given to her and she, in turn, had given to so many people across the world.

Patience is a bitch, grab the bull by the horns.

Portia stood from the chair, clenching the cell phone in her hand and walked through the house to the foyer where her purse and car keys sat on a table by the front door.

It was almost ten-thirty at night and she had no idea where Ethan lived. But she did know where he worked, so she'd start there.

The Game Changers Bar and Grill was popping with energy on a Friday night. From the moment Portia stepped inside, the sound of music and lots of people talking greeted her. A line of four people stood in front of her as she waited to speak to the hostess who was dressed in black pants and a black shirt, The Game Changers logo scrawled in red on this one.

Portia looked around while the lyrics to one of her favorite songs filtered through the air. She hummed along with P!nk's *F**kn Perfect* and admired the modern stylish and sleek look of this place. Instead of wall-to-wall sports memorabilia plain wood booths and chairs, and cracked peanut shells on the floor, there were floor to ceiling windows, rich mahogany wood walls and floors, high-boy tables with red leather cushioned chairs and a bar that stretched from one end of the main dining room to the other.

Just beyond the hostess booth were red carpeted stairs blocked off by a red rope. The bar was bathed in hazy red lighting, and along the top of each wall, a black and white digital sports and world news ticker ran. Across the room were the dark wood butcher block tables, some long enough to accommodate groups of eight, others cozy enough for a couple. Portia thought there might be booths toward the back, but couldn't really see because of the number of people either seated at the tables or at the bar. There was another area off to one side where a red, white and blue sign that read The Bullpen, hung. More seating was offered in that area where she could see computer stations, which she thought was an oddity in a sports bar, but admitted to being intrigued.

"Welcome to Game Changers, where your wish is the name of the game! How many are in your party tonight?"

The hostess was cheerful and had a beautiful smile of straight white teeth against her rich mocha complexion.

"Hi! Just one, please. Um, at the bar is fine," Portia told her.

After surveying the room, she was certain that being seated at the bar would offer the best view of the place.

"Sure. There are some seats at the other end, if you just head straight back. Enjoy the game!" the hostess exclaimed.

Her name was Joy, as stated by the silver name badge on the opposite side of the restaurant name, and she wore her hair in black with a few strategically placed bold red goddess braids.

"Thank you," Portia replied and walked past the hostess stand.

Across from the bar, the majority of the wall was covered by rows of flat screen televisions that all played some sports game or programming. It reminded her of an electronics store. Dishes clanked somewhere in the distance and the murmur of conversations followed her as she progressed deeper into the room. There was an energetic vibe here that she immediately liked. She bumped into someone, muttered an "excuse me" and kept moving until she spotted a seat at the bar.

Three bartenders were working the part of the crowd that faced them here, taking orders, fixing drinks and stopping to chat. Portia situated her small crossbody purse in her lap and snatched up a menu. She'd eaten earlier but knew that because she didn't drink often, she definitely needed something else on her stomach if she was even going to consider one of the adventurously described drinks.

"Hey there! What can I get for you tonight?" the bartender that came to a stop in front of her asked.

He was a tall and handsome guy. His rich sepia complexion and smiling eyes an added bonus to his muscular physique.

"I think I'll start off slow with a mojito and an order of fried mozzarella," she told him.

He nodded, smiled and continued to stare at her.

She didn't know what else to say so she looked away, staring toward the area called the Bullpen and guessing that it was their version of an internet bar within the sports bar. She was thinking that was a smart idea and had begun bobbing her head to the beat of Mark Ronson and Bruno Mars' *Uptown Funk*, when she glanced back behind the bar to see the bartender still staring at her. He'd moved about five people down from where she sat and he was actually working on another drink order, but each time he lifted his gaze from what he was doing, it was to stare at her.

Looking away once more, Portia wondered if Ethan was even here tonight. Her drink came in the next few minutes, followed by her food, and then a pretty woman with a warm smile. The woman was dressed in an outfit similar to the hostess's but wore her brown and honey blonde streaked hair straight with long bangs.

"Hi, I'm Camy Greer," she said, yelling slightly to be heard above the music. "You probably don't remember me because I was two years behind you in school. But I'm Del and Lance's sister."

As a result of the years that she'd been giving speaking engagements and talking with people before and after her sessions, Portia had immediately smiled upon Camy's greeting. "Hello. Yes, you were the singer," she replied. "You sang at the end of the year talent show in school the year I graduated."

Camy immediately nodded, her smile widening. "Right! I did. I was just a sophomore then and that was the first time I'd sung at school."

"But you also sang in church," Portia said, remembering the Sunday morning she'd gone to the small Baptist church by herself. "I remember you had a beautiful voice." While Portia liked to sing too, she was well aware of squawking bird sound her voice actually was.

"Thank you. And you remember my brother Lance?" Camy asked as she motioned behind the bar.

"Hi Portia."

The bartender had returned and Portia realized now why he'd been staring at her. Upon closer look, beyond the thick beard and wavy black hair, she did recognize him. He'd bulked up a bit and seemed to be taller than she recalled, but yes, this was Delancey Greer, one of Ethan's close friends.

"Hi Lance," she said. "It's good to see you."

It wasn't. Because with seeing Lance, the uneasiness that used to cloak her whenever she walked down the hall and saw Ethan with his crew, began to creep up inside her.

"I was surprised to hear you were back in town trying to sell

Sunnydale," Camy said. "But then I remembered it's your godmother's house."

"Yes. It is," Portia replied.

News always did travel fast in Providence and just because she'd been keeping a low profile around town, didn't mean that nobody noticed she was here. She picked up her glass and took a sip before replying.

"It's getting crowded down here, so let's grab your stuff. There's better seating upstairs," Camy said.

Portia didn't miss the look that passed between the siblings, but decided to ignore it. She should've just sent Ethan a text message and waited for his reply. Coming here tonight may have been a mistake. But she was here now and acting as normal as possible was probably the best route to take. Camy picked up the plate with her food and Portia grabbed her drink before slipping off the stool. Lance smiled at her as she left the bar. She followed Camy through the dining room the same way she'd come before and up the steps that had been roped off.

It was lively up here too, but there was a more relaxed atmosphere than had been downstairs. Portia also noted that there were mostly guys up here with the exception of some staff. Camy moved easily through the people, past the section of couches and lounge chairs toward another bar, where she finally saw him.

Ethan moved with ease back and forth as he fixed a drink, delivered it to someone sitting at the bar, laughed at something that was said and then began fixing another drink. Tonight, he wore a black t-shirt with a red oval shaped logo comprised of a baseball, basketball, football and soccer ball with the words Game Changers printed around the edges. The shirt molded to his muscular frame. The dark color a stark contrast to his buttery light complexion. His low-cut hair waved at the top and lay down smoothly on the sides. Defined biceps peeked from beneath the sleeve of his shirt, as her gaze traveled down muscled arms to settle on the gold watch at his wrist. As they approached the bar, she could hear his laughter and saw the light as it hit his eyes that appeared a more brilliant green tonight. She sucked in a breath and released it slowly as Camy led her to a seat at the end of the bar and set her plate on the bar top.

"You'll get great service up here," Camy said with a smile as she turned back to Portia.

"Thanks," Portia replied and was fairly certain she saw a devilish gleam in Camy's brown eyes.

Taking another sip from her glass, Portia eased onto the bar stool and slowly picked up a piece of the fried mozzarella to take a bite. She was halfway finished before he approached her.

"Didn't expect to see you here," Ethan said.

He was standing the same distance away from her as Lance had downstairs, yet there was a noticeably different reaction to him than she'd had to the other man. Her body had immediately warmed. The smile that had come easy to Lance and Camy, was slow forming now as she wasn't quite sure how to react around him after their night on the phone. But then Ethan did something unexpected.

He leaned over the bar to touch her hand. "I'm glad you came," he told her with a smile Portia believed was designed to have women all over the world dropping their panties on command.

She couldn't drop hers because there were just too many eyes here tonight, but damn, she certainly wanted to. Especially when his thumb slid to the palm of her hand circling slowly.

Portia swallowed the flash of trepidation at being here and having him touch her again. She squared her shoulders and replayed her godmother's words in her mind one more time. *Patience is a bitch, grab the bull by the horns.*

"I want you to show me how it's done," she said quickly.

"Show you how what's done?" he asked.

"Pleasure," she replied. "Show me how to experience pleasure."

The words coming from her mouth would've sounded odd to her agent, editor or any of the millions of people who'd ever attended one of her sessions or purchased and viewed her videos. The instructor asking to be taught. But Portia didn't care. A big part of her was screaming now or never, and she wasn't going to second guess it anymore.

The smile Ethan gave her was absolutely wicked and caused a familiar throbbing in her pussy.

"I'll show you everything," he replied and lifted her hand to his lips for a soft kiss.

$\mathcal{E}$verything began the moment Noah, Lance, Del, Rock and Jeret said goodnight. It was well after two in the morning by the time the bar cleared of all its customers and was cleaned to the guys' satisfaction. Portia had at first watched with fascination at the collaboration between them and their staff as they worked to bring the place back to order after a very busy night. Then, feeling like a heel for not helping, she'd grabbed a broom that had been set on the side when one of the servers ran back downstairs for something else, and began to sweep the floor. She'd swept, wiped down the couches and stools with a damp cloth and loaded glasses into the dishwasher behind the bar as if she worked at Game Changers. And when Lance joked about getting her a t-shirt for her next shift, Portia laughed, enjoying the easy way in which this group had seemed to accept her. This time.

"Sit down," she heard Ethan say.

He'd walked downstairs with the others to lock up after they'd filed out of the building. Portia could see down the stairs that the lights had been turned off on the lower level. Up here, the lights on the side of the cigar bar and in the center of the room were also off. He was telling her to sit on the stool at the bar where she'd sat when she first came up here hours ago. She did as he asked.

He went behind the bar to pick up a remote control and pushed some buttons on it. In seconds music blared throughout the room once more. This time it was a slower tune, a sexy song that she immediately recalled. Destiny's Child *Cater 2 U* was one of the many songs burned on the slow jams CDs that Portia played as a teenager each night she lay in her bed to go to sleep. Those nights when she'd dreamed of having the courage to perform the same erotic dance that the members of the singing group had in their video, with Ethan.

He came around the bar and buried his hands in her hair when he stood next to her. The feel of his blunt-tipped nails scraping over her scalp was sexy as hell and sent tingles of pleasure cascading down her body.

"Chapter 8," he whispered and lowered his face to hers. "Touch. Intimacy can be deepened through the art of touching."

Her words. Ethan was once again reciting her words to her. They were familiar and at the same time unknown. Spoken in his voice, they were erotic and mesmerizing.

He cupped her face, tilting her head slightly so that she seemed to be waiting for his kiss.

"I've wanted to touch you for longer than I can remember," he told her.

"Why?" she whispered and then quickly licked her lips. "I mean, why didn't you? Back then when we were younger?"

"I didn't know how," he told her. "Or if I should."

That was nonsense. In Portia's book Ethan had known how to do everything. He'd always been so self-assured and courageous. Those were just a few traits that had drawn her to him.

"Now," he said, his gaze falling to her lips, then lifting back to her eyes. "I do."

"Then do it," she said and heard the almost pleading sound of her voice. "Touch me, Ethan." Because she really didn't want to play any games or waste any more time. She wanted his hands on her, consequences be damned.

He moved his hands to slide along the line of her neck, rest on her shoulders and then move down her arms. When they came back up, he was unfastening the top buttons of the short sundress she wore. The feel of his strong fingers as they brushed along her skin was like heaven and when he had the three buttons undone and dipped a hand beneath the material to cup her breast, she sighed. It was the touch she'd dreamed about and so much more. The warmth that immediately soared through her body was indescribable and the knowledge of him holding her in his hand was intoxicating.

He wasn't giving her words tonight. He was simply touching her, just as she'd described in her book. Wrapping her mind around the concept she'd written being put to action on her may have been the most erotic thing she'd ever experienced.

When he'd massaged each breast, giving equal time to each aching mound and their now stiff nipples, his hands moved to her waist. She gasped when he suddenly lifted her from the stool and turned her so that he could sit her on the bar. Her hands dropped to his strong shoulders, kneading them through the material of his shirt. There was more to Ethan than brute strength, she knew that. Had seen it tonight as he'd interacted with his friends and their customers. Yet the feel of his taut muscles beneath her hands was enticing, arousing.

Ethan flattened his palms on her thighs. They were half covered by the material of her dress, but a part of his skin touched hers. He moved his hands slowly, pushing the material up until it bunched at her waist. In a quick motion that she was certain he'd practiced before, he removed her panties, dropping the wisp of silk onto the stool where she'd been sitting. His hands rested on her thighs again.

The song changed to Usher's *Burn* just as Ethan moved his hands upward. His thumbs rubbed along her inner thighs as he applied enough pressure to have Portia spreading her legs wider. When there was no place else to go, he used the pads of his thumbs to press against the plump folds between her legs. She couldn't help it; she squeezed his arms then yanked her hands away to rest them on the bar behind her as she lifted slightly to his touch.

His head was bent as he looked down at her. Heat infused her cheeks at the knowledge that he was staring at the most intimate part of her. His thumbs moved up and down the smoothly shaved skin for endless moments before finally parting her folds. Cool air hit her sensitive skin just seconds before Ethan pressed the pad of one thumb to her exposed clit. Portia almost leapt from the bar at that moment, her scream echoing along with the music as desire so quick and sharp caused her body to quake.

On a ragged moan, Ethan lowered his head and replaced his thumb with his tongue. For Portia, it was over when it had only really just begun. Her entire body trembled at the touch of his moist, hot tongue to the tight bud of her clit. An orgasm so strong it knocked the wind out of her then ricocheted throughout her body and left her panting.

But Ethan didn't stop.

He moved his tongue masterfully over her clit, up and down her slit and to her waiting core, as he had when he'd kissed her mouth. Her fingers gripped the smooth surface of the bar as her legs shook around him. And just when Portia thought she would definitely come again, Ethan pulled back.

He looked up at her, green eyes blazing with the same heat that roared through her body.

"Stop me now," he said raggedly. "If you've had enough, or if you're done here. Stop. Me. Now."

Permission. Another topic she discussed in her book with regard to intimacy and pleasure. The acquiescence of each partner came first with permission.

"Don't stop," she said with a shake of her head. "Please, don't stop."

Ethan moved quickly then, undoing the buckle of the belt at his waist and the button of his pants. Portia heard the rasp of his zipper easing down just as another song came on. This one was what her godmother had called an oldie but goodie, Prince's *Adore*. She wondered briefly how Ethan knew all the songs she'd listened to while dreaming of him, but then she heard the tear of a condom packet and her mind was immediately back to the here and now.

Her gaze dropped to see that he'd removed his shoes, jeans and boxers and now stood with his erection jutting forward just beneath the hem of his black shirt. She wanted to reach out and touch him, to feel his hot hardness in her hands, but he sheathed himself quickly with the condom. When he was done, he wrapped an arm around her waist, pulling her to the edge of the bar before crashing his lips into hers.

This kiss was pure heat. Like molten lava pouring slowly into her, each stroke of his tongue ramped up the temperature in the room. Her hands went around his neck, flattened on the back of his head and held him there. He sucked her tongue and she gasped at the blatant eroticism of the act. She pressed her aching breasts against his chest and moaned in a way that she hoped translated her need for more.

With one arm tightly around her waist, the other at her back, Ethan eased Portia off the bar top. He turned them slightly and just when Portia thought he was going to sit her on the stool again, he moved her only until the tip of his cock pressed firmly against her opening. She'd wrapped her legs around his waist, locking her ankles in place, as he pressed into her. She was tight and he was thick. The pleasure pain sensation spiraled through her as he pushed deeper inside, until their bodies were locked together.

He tore his mouth away from hers at that moment and groaned as he rested his forehead on hers. Portia closed her eyes, letting the feel of his thickness throbbing inside her resonate. She was just accepting that Ethan Henley was buried to the hilt inside of her when he began to move. Driving into her hard and fast, he pumped fiercely. She dug her low-cut nails into his shoulders through his shirt. She arched her back and let her head fall back as wave after wave of glorious pleasure overtook her.

And minutes later, when she came this time, Ethan was right there with her. His thrusts came slower as he slammed into her those final times before a gut-wrenching moan ripped from his throat. She was in her own hazy vortex of pleasure, but she held on tightly to Ethan and to this moment. She opened her eyes in time to see his face contorted with a mixture of glorious relief and a sense of wonder that she believed mimicked her own. He stumbled back, sitting on a bar stool and still holding her close. Their bodies remained connected, her legs still around his waist, his dick still inside of her as Ethan rested his head on her chest and Portia held him there. She closed her eyes and wished, as she had so many times before, that this was real. That it was forever. That her dreams had finally come true.

Ethan closed the door to his truck and circled around to the sidewalk where Portia was already standing. Suddenly she looked young and vulnerable again, like when they were in school. A small purse sat at her hip, and the black strap crossing over her chest was darker against the short light purple dress she wore. Her shoes were flat and she'd pulled her curly mass of hair back into a ponytail while she was in her car. It had been out and wild as he'd held her in his arms, pumping into her with every bit of desire that had been swirling inside of him.

Coming to a stop in front of her, Ethan couldn't help but think of what they'd just done at the bar. Hell, he hadn't been able to stop thinking about it since she'd eased off his lap and hurried to the bathroom. Minutes later they'd both come out of separate bathrooms together and stood in the small hallway staring oddly at each other. He hadn't known exactly what to say to her, since sex at the bar had been the farthest thing from his mind tonight. Yet it happened, and he wasn't a bit sorry about that.

"Thanks for following me home," she said after clearing her throat.

"It's late," he told her. "I would've preferred to drive you myself, but as long as I can make sure you're safe, I'm cool with it."

She nodded and silence ensued once more.

It shouldn't be this weird. Ethan had been with plenty of women before and a good number of them had been one-night stands. There'd never been this type of uncomfortable silence. Probably because he'd always been sure to set the ground rules before any action could take place. He hadn't been able to do that with Portia and wondered if now was too late.

"I'm leaving Monday night," she said abruptly. "Rod says the work will be complete by then and my book tour continues on Tuesday."

"Where does the tour continue?" Ethan asked because he didn't know how else to respond. He'd known that she wasn't in Providence to stay, and up until this moment that had been fine by him. Now, he wasn't sure how to react.

He should've felt relieved. There was no need to have a

conversation about no strings, just sex, if she was leaving in a couple of days. But that's not what he felt at all.

"New York," she answered. "Then Boston before I head back to the West Coast. It's a seven-week tour which will end in Portland and then I'll head back home to Seattle."

"You live in Seattle?"

"Yes."

He frowned. "I didn't know that."

"I know," she said with a nod.

It was almost four o'clock in the morning and they were standing on the sidewalk in front of the brightest colored house on the block sharing small talk.

"You should get inside. It's pretty late."

"Yes, it is." She took a big enough breath that he could see her shoulders rise and fall with the exhale. "Thanks again...for everything."

Ethan shook his head. "Stop thanking me," he said. It was making him feel very uncomfortable.

She'd thanked him when his cheek was pressed against her chest and he'd been trying to catch his breath after that whirlwind orgasm. The words had been quiet and he presumed she thought he hadn't heard them because seconds later she'd moved off his lap. But he'd heard, and the words made him feel like they'd just completed a sex-for-hire transaction. Now she was thanking him for seeing her home, as if she didn't expect him to have that much decency, and it was irritating the hell out of him.

He stepped closer and took her hand, staring down at it for a few seconds before moving up the walkway. She followed without a word, coming up onto the porch. If this were the end of a real date—and not so late at night—this may have been the time for the goodnight kiss. She would go into the house and he would get into his truck and head home. Maybe there would be a call the next day to schedule another date, or maybe not. There probably would be another date because Ethan felt like he definitely wanted to see Portia again.

"Get home safely," she said as she pulled her hand from his and opened the screen door.

The handle was fixed now, and she quickly found her key and opened the front door. She was stepping inside the house by the time Ethan found his next words.

"See you later," he told her.

Her response was a curt nod and a small smile before she ducked inside and closed the door behind her. Ethan cursed all the way down the steps and the walkway to his truck at his stupidity. *See you later.* Who even said that anymore? And what the hell did it mean? Was he going to call her tomorrow and ask her out on another—well, a real date? Or would he just pop over here again with some other excuse to see her?

He slammed the door upon getting into his truck, started the engine and pulled off knowing there was a high probability that he wouldn't do any of those things. And there was no need in feeling guilty if tonight had been their one-night stand, because Portia wasn't here to stay. It was working out perfectly.

Even though he lay in his bed twenty minutes later feeling the same longing to hear her voice and to touch her as he had last night and the night before.

9

"*H*ey there! Long time, no see."

On Sunday afternoon, Portia looked up from the spot where she'd been sitting on the front lawn going through a box of CDs to see Camy Greer.

"Oh, hi," she replied.

Camy's smile was genuine as she lifted her sunglasses from her face to prop them on top of her head. She wore white shorts and a pink tank top as she knelt down across from Portia.

"So it was nice to see you last night at the bar. I was just driving past on my way from the store and saw you out here," she continued.

"The bar was a change of scenery for me," Portia said. "I'm glad I went."

She was more than glad she'd decided to go to Game Changers last night because, it had, in essence, been a game changer for her. It was the first time in her life that she'd had a rewarding sexual experience. She'd thought about that fact all morning and now well into early afternoon.

"Good. If you're not too busy around here today, I'd like to invite you over to my place. I'm having a cookout so there'll be lots of food and drinks and just casual company."

Casual company and an invitation to a cookout at someone's house. More things Portia had daydreamed about while growing up here. She'd brought these boxes outside to go through because the smell of fresh paint inside the house was giving her a headache. But while picking through each item she'd been flanked by more memories than she could handle. Memories of her time in Providence, of the loneliness that she thought would someday kill her and the things she'd used to try to keep her sanity.

She'd thought things would change once she got to college, but for the most part it was still the same. There'd been no pledging sororities for her. A group of girls judging her on any number of things wasn't really her idea of friendship, and while she could accept that for some people the experience was much different and bonds were made in those groups, she hadn't been willing to try. Her mostly solitary status continued as she finally found a home in Seattle and after a while she'd started to think it wasn't so bad.

After being gone for twelve years, she'd been back in Providence for a little over a week and she'd not only had sex with her high school crush, but was now being invited to an event she was fairly certain Ethan and his friends would also be attending.

"Come on, say yes," Camy prodded. "It's a beautiful day and we're going to have so much food and music. Lance wrote this song and I'm going to sing it and then we'll maybe play some cards or just sit around eating and drinking until we're ready to fall asleep."

She laughed and Portia smiled. Camy had always been outgoing and cheerful. While Portia hadn't spent as much time at the church, in the school chorus or in any of the other circles Camy had run in, she recalled seeing Camy around town a lot and admiring her for the way she made it look as if being friends with someone was so easy. Portia had Sunny and her college roommate who'd married and moved to Germany with her military husband, but that was it. Back in Seattle, her relationship with her downstairs neighbor was pretty cordial, but she wasn't totally sure she'd call Bethany a close friend.

"I should really get this packing done," she replied to Camy and watched as the woman's mouth turned down at the corners.

"Girl, you don't want to sit here all day working. I can see it in your eyes. You're itching to get up from here and do something fun. Lucky for you that I came along," Camy told her.

Camy also took that moment to reach into the box and pull out a CD. "This is the old Mariah Carey. I used to love this CD. I sang *Vision of Love* so much my mother wanted to hurl me and my CD player out the window. I know I was just a baby when this released, but my mother always said I was an old soul."

Portia heard the hint of sadness in Camy's voice as she said those last words. Roxanne Greer had been sick for as long as Portia could remember. By the way Camy was staring with a mixture of grief and fond memories at the CD, Portia assumed Roxanne had passed away during the years she'd been gone.

"Well you and I were a lot alike because I migrated toward older music too. There are so many CDs here," Portia said. "I'd forgotten all about them. But I remember all the nights listening to slow songs before falling asleep."

She also recalled the songs that played through the speakers at the bar last night when she'd been with Ethan.

"You should bring them with you to the cookout. It'll be fun to reminisce a bit. And we could have our own karaoke night. I keep trying to tell the guys they should have one down at the bar, but Lance is stuck on the playlists they use on loop or live entertainment," Camy said, excitement once again in her tone.

"I don't know about all that." She decided she liked Camy

excited and enthusiastic, instead of sad. "But I'll come to the cookout to hear the new song you're going to sing."

"Great! You remember where our house is right? The rambling old colonial down by the bridge. Just show up around five or sooner if you're inclined to help me with some of the food." She stood, but then knelt again and grabbed the Mariah Carey CD. "Can I keep this? I want to listen to it in the car while I finish running my errands."

"Sure. And I'll come early to help. I just have to clean up this mess here first," she told her and watched as Camy danced her way across the grass to her car.

Feeling a little lighter than she had just moments before, Portia began picking up the stacks of CDs and placing them neatly into the box she'd taken them out of earlier. This time as she moved, she hummed one of Mariah Carey's tunes and felt the bits of happiness she'd been deprived of when she was a young girl collecting all this music.

Wayne and Judy did not like loud music being played in the house. That meant if they could walk past her closed bedroom door and hear the music, it was too loud. Wayne insisted on Portia remaining focused on getting perfect grades so that she would receive scholarships and acceptance letters to all the Ivy League colleges. Even though he'd already decided she was going to Yale. It was her mother's job to make sure this happened, so Judy was stern about Portia's extracurricular activities and her social life—meaning she basically had none. Sure, she could go to the library after school or to do anything that centered around academics but that was about it. There'd been a schedule on the back of Portia's bedroom door and Portia dare not alter it because that would place her directly on the receiving end of Judy's wrath.

The only place Portia was allowed to go with permission was here, to Sunnydale. All the kids in school referred to Sunny's yellow Victorian by that name. It could've also come about because of the friendly neighbor Sunny was. While she was strict about not letting the busybodies of this town—as she called them —through her front door to feed their gossip mill, it wasn't strange to see her sitting on her front porch with fresh baked cookies and lemonade for the children as they walked by on their way home from school. Portia always thought Sunny would've been a terrific mother. Except Sunny had been clear that men were only good for one thing and once they'd shown her all their tricks in bed, she politely moved on to the next one. And yet she'd talked to Portia last night of finding love.

With a shake of her head to clear that thought from her mind, Portia stood and paused before lifting the box to take back inside. She looked at the lovely yellow house with the gray shutters and realized with a start that every happy moment she'd ever had during her childhood had happened in there. Not in the house she'd shared with her parents, or the schools she'd spent the bulk of her time in, or even the church where older women whispered behind her back just as much as the young girls. Every fond part of Providence for Portia was at Sunnydale. And in a couple of days she would sign the paperwork to sell it to someone else.

Portia didn't know how she felt about that and she didn't have much time to consider it either. She had a couple more boxes to go through before she wanted to shower and change and head over to Camy's house. It was her first social invitation in Providence. It didn't matter that it'd come years too late, she was still excited about receiving it, partly because she knew Ethan would be there.

Ethan's fingers paused over the screen of his phone.

She hadn't responded to his text messages.

Three of them and no answer.

He was trying not to feel rejected. There were plenty of other numbers stored in his phone that he could dial if he wanted a repeat of last night. Except, he knew it wouldn't actually be a repeat because it wouldn't be with Portia. He had a feeling there was never going to be another Portia in his life. He didn't even know why he was thinking of her in that way. She was only here for another couple of days and then she'd be gone. That worked perfectly because another monogamous relationship was out of the question for him. Once was enough, especially when it ended with him dangerously close to using his training to actually kill someone.

It had been months since he'd thought about the six years he'd spent in D.C. working for the Secret Service. He'd accomplished a goal nobody in this town thought he would, obtaining a college degree and a good government job. He was in the place he'd imagined himself being after the rough childhood he'd endured. And in one afternoon, it had all come crashing down.

With a frown, Ethan tucked the phone into his pocket and got out of his truck. He opened the back-passenger door and pulled out three cases of beer he'd taken from the bar and headed toward the backyard of Camy's house. It used to be Del and Lance's home too, until the vandalism incident at the school where neither of the twins would tell who had trashed the boys' locker room and the gym teachers' offices. That had been the last straw for their mother and off to the House they went. Ethan had been there for almost a year at that time and had bonded with the twins in a way he'd never done with any of the other residents.

The three of them used to walk by this two-story white house with its black shutters and sprawling front and back lawns on many occasions. In fact, Del and Lance always spent Sunday afternoons here with their mother and Camy. Now, Ethan walked toward the back of the house where the large yard had been freshly landscaped. The grass was cut, the bushes trimmed and fresh mulch was around each of the mature trees. Camy took pride in keeping the house up, inside and out, especially since she was the only one who lived there now.

Del was already standing at one of the two grills set up closest to the house. White tents stood over two picnic tables with benches on each side. There were more chairs positioned around the tents and two big red coolers sitting beside a tree. Ethan moved in that direction to set the cases of beer down beside the coolers. He'd just ripped the paper wrapping off one and was about to start loading the cans into one of the coolers when Lance appeared.

"Guess who's coming today?" he asked, but Ethan assumed he was talking to Del and didn't bother to turn around and answer.

"Okay, you don't want to guess. Well, I'll tell you because I don't think you'll want to be as surprised as you were when you saw her last night."

Now, he did turn toward where Lance was standing.

The smile that spread across Lance's face was big and annoying. "Yeah, I thought that'd get your attention."

"You think you could help unload my truck or you wanna keep yapping?" Ethan asked and went back to taking the beers out of the package and dropping them into the ice inside the cooler.

"Sure. You're probably going to need a cold one when you see Portia. She looks even hotter than she did last night, if that's possible."

Ethan kept working.

"She's in the house right now, helping Camy in the kitchen. Isn't she, Del? And man, those shorts she's wearing are really short. I mean, they're shorter than the dress she wore last night and that was short. You know what I'm sayin—"

His words were cut short when Del came over and bowed

him in the ribs playfully. "Stop teasing him. It's cool if he's got a thing for little Portia."

"She's not little," Ethan snapped before he could stop himself.

Del gazed at Ethan with a slow grin. "I can agree with that," Del said. "She's definitely all grown up now. Easy to see why she's in the sex industry."

"What the hell does that mean?" Ethan asked.

He'd been keeping the eye contact to a minimum while opening another pack of beer.

"Nothing, man. Don't bite my head off," Del said. "We're just messing with you. She seems like a really nice woman, who happens to be extremely attractive and pretty rich too. Her company's called Pleasure, Inc. and it's made a killing over the past few years. Her book's even on track to become a bestseller."

Irritated that Del had investigated Portia, Ethan looked up to his friend with a frown. Sure, he'd run her name and dug up a few things about her too. And his friend, Byran at the Secret Service had found her private cell phone number. But Ethan hadn't thought he was being intrusive. Del, on the other hand, had no reason to want to know more about Portia.

"She's a successful businesswoman," Ethan replied. "No need for you to dig up anything else about her."

Del shrugged. "She's been gone a while and now she's back. I wanted to know why."

So had Ethan. The three of them each had law enforcement experience so being precautious and suspicious came natural to them.

"Yeah, she's back alright, and looking sweeeeet," Lance said. "Still, I never really figured you'd go for her, E. I mean, you never did when we were in school."

"She was two years younger than us," Del said. "Considering where we were forced to live, we were all trying to stay in our lane then."

"Yeah, she's still two years younger than us," Lance stated.

"But she's an adult now," Ethan told them.

He stood, lifting the empty boxes in his hand. He could take them into the house. Camy kept a recycling bin right outside the pantry. There was also one on the side of the house near the trash cans. But he was not going inside just to see Portia.

"An adult that you're definitely looking at with interest," Lance continued. "Camy told me how your eyes almost bugged out of your head when she brought Portia upstairs last night. And we noticed the two of you stayed behind to "clean up" a little more after we all left." Lance used his fingers to make air quotes, annoying the hell out of Ethan.

"Cut it out," Ethan told him. "There's nothing there." At least that's what he'd been desperately trying to convince himself.

"I can't tell," Lance insisted, and Ethan wanted to punch him.

Del just shook his head. "Don't let him get to you, E. You know how big of an ass he can be."

"Yeah." They all knew that about Lance, unfortunately, this time, the guy had managed to latch onto something that Ethan just didn't want to address. He was about to turn and head toward the house, but Lance stopped him with his next comment.

"It's cool if you've got a thing for Portia." Lance stared at Ethan seriously. "I told you that when we were in school, but you ignored me. You know I don't hold with the rules other people make. If you liked her and she liked you, there should've never been a problem. And if you want to go for it with her now, that makes perfect sense."

There wasn't a problem, Ethan thought. He hadn't pursued Portia back then because he hadn't known what he felt for her. It had always been different with her. He knew what he wanted from the other girls, and he knew how to get it. With Portia, not so much. She wasn't like other girls and not just by outside appearances. There was something inside her, a kindness and purity that he hadn't sensed in anybody else. What was a guy like him going to do with someone like that?

"Look, let's be clear," Ethan said. "I don't have a thing for Portia. I don't plan on having a thing for anyone, anytime soon. Now, can you move your talkative ass out to the truck and get some of those boxes?"

He didn't wait for Lance's response, but turned around, ready to walk out of the yard and back to his truck. Instead, he walked straight into Portia, who had apparently been standing right behind him.

Her hair was pulled up so that her curls hung in a cheerful tail down to her shoulders. Portia's denim shorts weren't short. The light washed out denim came to her knees but had rips strategically placed so that the shorts looked both distressed and sexy as hell. A simple gray tank top hugged her perfect palm-sized breasts and she was smiling at him. It was a stilted smile, but still one that made him feel like a colossal ass for what he'd just said regarding her.

She looked great but that didn't explain the clenching in his chest when he saw her. "Hey," was all Ethan could manage to say because hell if he knew what was going on between them.

Portia lifted a hand and waved her fingers. "Hey."

"Ah, we've got boxes to get from the truck," Del said and reached over to yank his twin by the arm. "Let's go get 'em."

Lance nodded. "Yeah. Let's do that."

The two of them leaving did nothing to make Ethan feel better, although it probably should have. Hadn't he been thinking of being alone with Portia again all day? Isn't that the real reason he'd been so irritated with her not answering his text messages?

"I sent you a text," he said because he couldn't think of anything else that wouldn't make him sound more like an idiot.

The slight furrow of her forehead wasn't exactly the reaction he'd expected.

"You did?" she asked and then reached into her back pocket to pull out her phone.

"Yeah, just once," he started and resisted the urge to smack himself on the forehead for sounding like a bumbling teenager. "Or maybe twice. I just wanted to see how you were doing today."

"Three times," she said still staring down at her phone screen.

"Huh?"

She looked up at him. "You sent three text messages."

Now would be a good time for a hole to open in the earth and swallow him as a reprieve from the embarrassment he was feeling right now.

Portia shook her head as she looked down again and her fingers moved over the phone. "I put my phone on silent this morning after speaking to my agent. The publishing house isn't happy that I'm not back in New York yet, but I reassured them that I'd be there next Tuesday for the scheduled signings. My agent said the book was doing great, but they want me on the road to keep the momentum going. I didn't feel like explaining myself over and over again, so I just silenced the phone for a while. Sorry about that." She looked at him again with another smile.

This one was more genuine. It lifted her cheekbones and showcased the golden flecks in her eyes. Ethan swallowed hard before speaking because a little bit of that worry he'd seen in her previously was gone.

"No problem," he said and shifted from one foot to the other. "And ah, about what I said…I mean, what you may have heard. I was just, ah…it wasn't—"

She shook her head again. "No worries, Ethan. I don't have a thing for you either. And last night, well, that was great. I'm totally fine with great sex, especially since I'd never had it until you."

Fuck!

Now he felt even lower than the dirt beneath his feet. Sure, she'd just given him a huge compliment, but the hitch in her voice as she'd said those last words told more than anything he'd actually heard her say. Did she still have a thing for him? And if so, how did that effect the thing he'd had for her but had been too stupid to explore?

"You're reading my book, so I'm flattered," she continued. "And to be quite honest, I am actually enjoying the way you—I mean, we—have been able to implement the things I wrote into reality. It's what my work is all about."

So this was an experiment for her. Okay, that was cool. Ethan could get behind that. Experiments weren't permanent. There were no expectations beyond the question the project sought to answer. He nodded and lifted a hand to drag down the back of his head.

"Glad I can be of assistance," he said, for lack of a better response. And then, "I need a beer. How about you?"

She chuckled and for an instant, Ethan felt at ease. The sound seemed so natural and lit up her face. He should just relax. She obviously wasn't angry about his words, so why should he still feel uncomfortable about her having heard them? He had no idea and didn't want to waste any more time contemplating an issue, that apparently wasn't really an issue.

"Sure. How about I get us both a beer?" She'd moved around him and was reaching into the cooler he'd just filled while Ethan still stood there not knowing what to say.

He'd never been rendered speechless by a woman before. Well, that wasn't entirely true. His mother's actions had been something Ethan hadn't talked about for years after it had happened. And then there was Savannah. No, it seemed Ethan was well-versed in what women could do to him. Well-versed and wary, which made him even happier when he accepted the beer from Portia. He knew very well what to expect from women and wasn't about to take a walk down the path of disappointment again. So, it was good that Portia was on board with the temporary nature of whatever they were doing together.

Ethan pulled the top off the beer and took a deep drag.

It was damn good.

10

*Y*esterday had been perfect.

Portia smiled as her fingers stilled over the keys of her laptop. It was nearing noon on a dreary Sunday and she was sitting cross-legged on her childhood bed working on an outline for a book that would explore the emotional aspect of sexual attraction. The idea had come to her yesterday while she'd stood listening to Ethan talk to his friends.

He'd said he didn't have a thing for her, that he didn't plan to have a thing for anyone for a while. And with those words, Portia had felt like she was sixteen all over again. But this time, she'd actually heard the words. It was odd and she'd spent a good portion of the night thinking of just how weird her train of thought was, but when she'd climbed out of bed at almost nine this morning and headed for the shower, she'd had a moment of clarity. When she was in high school, she'd wanted Ethan Henley more than she'd wanted air. If Ethan had been a jerk like a good majority of the kids in Providence High, she wouldn't have wanted him at all. If he'd come to her and asked her on a date, and if she'd gone on that date and he'd touched her in any way, kissed her or acted as if he wanted to do something intimate with her, what would she have done? Would she have frozen? Run scared? Cry? Or embarrassed herself in some other way?

Probably, she'd thought just as the warm spray of water had burst from the showerhead to pepper her face. But now, so many years after she'd been through the ringer and back, when he'd read her book and started to teach her about intimacy via the words she'd written, Portia had been ready to learn. She'd been so ready that she'd sought him out at the bar and pushed aside any misgivings or inhibitions to allow the unimaginable to happen.

Emotions had run rampant through her all yesterday as she'd tried to sort through how she was supposed to feel about their interlude at the bar. And then when she'd seen him and heard his words, she'd known how she should feel. Just as he did. Like this was just a learning experience for her. Just as the awful break-up with Bobby and her retribution against him had been.

A bowl of fruit and two cups of coffee later, Portia had outlined half the book she wanted to write next. She'd made notes on the research she would need to do, some of which she'd already done but needed to delve a little further, but mainly she relied heavily on things she'd learned via her minor in psychology. Emotion springs from a complex state of feeling resulting in physical and psychological changes that influence thought and behavior. There were three main categories of motivation: physiological, neurological and cognitive. Right now, Portia was hung up on the physiological theory, which suggested that responses within the body were responsible for emotions. If that were one hundred percent true, then with each orgasm Ethan had brought her that night on the phone and at the bar, she should be well on her way to being in love with him. Or at the very least in lust.

Considering the fact that she couldn't stop thinking about how good the thickness of his cock felt deep inside her and how she really wanted to experience that feeling again, she would venture to say that theory was correct.

She'd told Ethan that she was game for good sex and that wasn't a lie. Had hearing him say he didn't have a thing for her hurt her feelings in any way? Of course it had. But Portia was no longer that girl who believed in fairy tale love and Ethan being her prince charming in a football uniform. She was an adult who had seen more and now knew more than she had back then. Her time in Providence was temporary and so was her time with Ethan. She was fine with that.

What Portia wasn't fine with, was the call she'd received from Rod at just about three o'clock in the afternoon.

"I can come by and board up the windows if you like," Rod said.

Portia had stopped writing when the phone rang and climbed off the bed to look out her window. The sky was a dusky gray color with clouds that looked as if they were going to explode at any moment. Tree branches bent with the wind and she could hear the screech of the swing on the porch moving back and forth.

"Storm's expected to make landfall sometime in the middle of the night. But things are going to get pretty dicey before then. I know you're there by yourself, so I was thinking of coming over just to help you batten down. Or maybe you'd rather head over to Clarice's motel for the night. At least you won't be alone there," Rod continued.

"No, I'll be fine," Portia told him. "And you don't have to come over. I'll take care of the house."

He'd asked about coming over again before inviting her to come over to his parents' house where he planned to ride out the storm with them, all of which Portia declined. She did turn on the television after disconnecting the call. She'd been so wrapped up in her research and outlining all day that she hadn't paid attention to anything that was going on around her.

She sat on the edge of the bed switching channels each time a commercial came on interrupting the news broadcasts. Hurricane Sylvie had formed near the Cape Verde Islands two weeks ago. In that time, the storm had steadily strengthened, reaching its peak as a Category 5 hurricane. The storm had reached the Outer Banks of North Carolina late last night and had now weakened to a Category 2 storm that was scheduled to hit the Virginia and D.C. area in a matter of hours.

Portia recalled the last time she'd experienced a hurricane. It had been a few years before she'd graduated from high school, when Hurricane Isabel had ravaged the East Coast. She immediately went downstairs into the kitchen to make sure she still had the bottles of water she'd purchased the day before yesterday. Her next trek was to find a flashlight and batteries, but she was stopped by her cell phone ringing again. She'd stuffed it into the pocket of the sweatpants she wore and now reached for it without looking at the screen.

"Storm's coming," Sunny said the moment she answered. "I heard on the radio that it's heading right for Providence."

"I know. I'm looking for flashlights now."

"In the kitchen drawer by the refrigerator," she said.

Portia sighed because she'd packed that box yesterday. "Okay. I'll get it."

"Stay away from the windows. The middle bedroom upstairs is the best place to get comfortable. There's a sleeping bag and blankets in one of the closets up there. Take your flashlights, water and snacks on up there and settle in for the night. The house is sturdy. It's been standing for almost two hundred years, it'll keep standing."

"Yes ma'am," Portia said as she continued moving throughout the house collecting things.

She'd grabbed her purse and the phone charger she'd left beside it this morning. There were only six of the waters left, so she dropped them into a plastic bag and carried that with her.

"Turn off all the lights and unplug everything. The power will probably go out, but you don't want any power surges when it clicks back on. You can keep your phone charged in the middle room until the power does go out," Sunny continued.

"Right," Portia said with a nod. She was just about to head upstairs again when there was a knock at the door.

She frowned because she figured it was Rod who hadn't listened to her tell him many times that he didn't need to come over.

"Are there batteries in the flashlight?" she asked Sunny. "Or someplace else in the house?"

"Should be in the same drawer," Sunny said. "But the flashlight is a sturdy one, it should go all night without having to be recharged. I sure am glad you're there in the house seeing this project through. Not tonight though, this storm seems like it's gonna be a nasty one."

Portia opened the door at that moment and was startled to see Ethan standing there. It must've started to rain because his shirt had huge wet spots on it, but that was the only thing off about his appearance. Otherwise he appeared tall, muscled and scrumptious as he stood there looking like something else that could possibly go all night. But that wasn't all, not tonight. Seeing Ethan standing on her porch when a storm was brewing outside made her feel something else. Important, cared-for, cherished. Things she'd never expected to feel from a man again.

Yesterday had been awful.

Ethan was of a mind to make today better. He'd finished his

PLAY TO WIN | 113

shift at the bar about an hour ago and stopped at the store before getting to his final destination. Sunnydale. Even if he hadn't already decided he needed to see Portia today, Camy coming into the bar stating quite succinctly that he needed to get his head out of his ass would possibly have prompted him to do so.

"You're being a jerk. She still likes you a lot," Camy had said.

"I was with her all evening," he'd replied. And it was true.

From the time that Portia had surprised him by standing right behind him while he talked about not having a thing for her, until somewhere around eleven-thirty when he'd followed her home, they hadn't been more than a few feet apart. She'd eaten and he had too. She'd laughed at Lance's silly jokes and arm wrestled with Rock, even though they all knew who was going to win. When Camy sang and Lance played the guitar, Portia had crossed her legs and leaned forward to rest an elbow on her thigh. She'd swayed to the music and Ethan had watched her feel every lyric of the ballad. So he'd had no idea how that equated to being a jerk.

"Why aren't you with her now? You know the hurricane is coming. She's all by herself in that big old house. What if she doesn't have enough water or something? What if the windows get blown in, or there's flooding?"

"Stop!" Ethan had said when it seemed like Camy's rambling would last forever. "You're in an old house by yourself too."

"Del and Lance are both coming over as soon as they close down the bar to board up the windows and do whatever else needs to be done before things get bad."

He was about to say something else, but she held up a hand to stop him.

"Yes. I could've done all those things myself. I don't *need* a man around to take care of things. And I'm sure Portia doesn't either. But, if there is a man who professes to care about a woman, they should be there to do those things. Chivalry's not dead." Camy finished with an arched brow that dared Ethan to say anything to the contrary.

"I've already got plans," Ethan told her at the risk of receiving more scathing looks. "And besides, she's still leaving soon, so I'm sure she's spending the day packing."

"I don't think she wants to leave," Camy continued.

Ethan moved away from the bar to return a stack of menus to the hostess stand.

"You should've seen the look in her eyes when she was going through the stuff in those boxes yesterday. I found her sitting on the front lawn, just like she used to do when she was younger. That's why I stopped and talked to her, because it sucks that nobody paid any attention to her before."

Her words weren't new to Ethan. He'd thought them a time or two during the time that Portia had been back in town.

"We were kids, Camy. We didn't realize what we were doing. And if we did, we were too young and dumb to stop. Portia understands that now."

"Does she?" Camy had asked.

Ethan was saved by Del who came along to tell them that the mayor had announced that everyone close and head home because the storm was getting closer. True to the plan he'd already concocted while working today, Ethan had left the bar and made a quick run to the market and hardware store that was running out of supplies.

Now he was standing on her front porch, mildly wet, holding bags in his arms and staring at perhaps the most attractive woman he'd ever seen.

She was clearly surprised to see him, as evidenced by the way her mouth instantly gaped open when she opened the door. Now, she was shaking her head and telling whoever was on the phone that she had to go and that yes, she would be okay during the storm, before disconnecting the call.

"Hi," Ethan said because he wasn't totally sure she knew what to say to his impromptu visit. "I picked up some things I thought you might be able to use."

He went with his gut and immediately began walking as if he intended to enter the house. Then something inside halted him and he stopped just a breath away from her. He looked down to see the question in her eyes as she tilted her head upward to meet his gaze. Once again, she appeared vulnerable in baggy gray sweatpants, sock covered feet and a t-shirt that hung off one shoulder. She wore no make-up and innocence in her gaze was enough to make him feel guilty about something, everything or hell, anything.

"Can I come in?" he asked, praying that she wouldn't say no.

She nodded and he almost sighed with relief.

He heard the door close behind him and looked over his shoulder to ask, "Which way to the kitchen?"

"Through the living room and the parlor," she said. "What did you buy?"

"Provisions," he answered. "We're in for a rough night. I'm going to put this stuff down and then I'll walk around and check the windows."

"They're new," she said just as he put the bags on the floor in the kitchen because there was no furniture.

"All the more reason to check on them. The wind's picking up already. Rod said there are some pieces of wood down in the basement. I'll just head down there to see what I can use."

"You called Rod and talked to him about my—this—house?" He didn't miss the surprise in her voice and it made him feel like an ass that she didn't think enough of him to know he'd look out for her.

He turned to her then, touching a finger to her chin. "I did. And after I get the windows situated, we can fix some dinner while we still have power and then buckle in for the night."

"You're staying here?"

"I am if that's alright with you." He desperately wanted her to say it was okay, but if she didn't, if she asked him to leave, he would. He'd hate and worry every second he wasn't with her during this storm, but he wouldn't push her in any way. After all she'd been through in this town, he wasn't going to make any more bad memories for her.

She stared at him for what seemed like endless seconds, contemplating no doubt. Probably asking if she could trust him? If this wasn't another cruel joke, or if it were a result of some type of guilt trip? Portia always seemed to have questions and there was a time when Ethan thought he'd had all the answers. Tonight, he was rethinking everything he thought he'd known about his feelings for Portia and why he'd chosen to stay away from her.

"That's fine with me," she answered finally.

His smile probably gave away the relief he felt, but he didn't mind. As long as he was here with her.

11

"'*The Act of Intimacy. At first it is an act because there has not been a chance for the new couple to get to know each other well enough for it to become a natural progression of the relationship. Therefore "acts" must occur to bring them closer to the intimacy they desire.'*"

"You memorized my book."

It wasn't a question, just a quiet statement as they sat on top of a sleeping bag on the floor of the middle room. Outside the wind had begun to howl, rattling against the windows as the storm grew closer.

"Not every word. Just specific parts," Ethan replied.

"Why?"

"Truth: it makes me feel closer to you," he said and then waited.

An hour ago, he'd fixed them grilled cheese sandwiches. Actually, he'd burned the sandwiches and Portia cooked them new ones while Ethan opened cans of tomato soup and warmed it on the stove. After eating, they cleaned the dishes and walked through the house unplugging everything, per Sunny's instructions. As if that act alone summoned the storm to become more powerful, the electricity went out as they'd walked up the stairs. She'd switched on the flashlight she'd stuffed in her pocket, but Ethan had another idea. He used the flashlight on his phone to head back downstairs and grabbed the candles he'd purchased from the store.

Now, those candles were lit all around the room so that they were sitting in the midst of a golden glow.

"Truth," she said abruptly. "I don't know how hearing you say that is supposed to make me feel."

"I don't know either, Portia. I just know that I've read your book three times already. I haven't read like that since college." He chuckled and she recalled how much she'd loved that sound.

"I always loved reading." That was probably a better thing to admit. She was sitting with her back against the wall, legs crossed at the ankle, hands in her lap. "I guess that's why writing was such an easy transition for me."

"And writing about intimacy, how did you get into that?" he asked the question that had been on his mind for days now. The book wasn't Portia's first foray into the sex industry. Her company Pleasure Inc. was behind an entire course of instructive videos that had not only made her rich, but also immensely popular within the industry.

She was quiet for long moments and Ethan wondered if he'd asked the wrong question. They were sitting so close that the sides of their bodies touched. His legs obviously stretched longer than hers on the sleeping bag. The candles around them burning brightly.

"It just happened," she eventually responded.

"I get it. Things just happen all the time." It was a lesson he'd learned on a couple of occasions. "Did you ever think you'd end up back here in Providence?"

She'd folded her hands in her lap and turned to look over at him. "No. I never wanted to come back."

"Because of how badly you were treated." He hated that he'd indirectly been a part of that. If he could get a do-over he'd take it, if only to make things better for her.

"Because of a lot of things. Not just your friends or other kids in school. I always felt out of place here."

"And when you went away to college you felt better? Because I thought I'd feel better once I was out of Providence too and for a while I did, but deep down inside I think I always knew I'd come back." That was the first time he'd ever admitted that to anyone.

She reached up to tuck thick curls back behind her ear. They sprung loose seconds after her hand moved and he grinned at the instant look of frustration that crossed her face. "You've always had a place here, Ethan. Whether it was on the high school football team or now, owning a bar. You and Del and the others, were an integral part of this town."

"Why? Because we were always accused of trying to tear it down?" That question may have been a bit harsh considering Portia wasn't one of the ones who'd accused him and his friends of doing everything except the right thing during their teenage years.

"I never believed all that stuff they said about you guys. I mean, sure I thought you were mean, inconsiderate jerks toward me. But I never thought you were dangerous."

She'd never know how much those words meant to him. That clenching in his chest he'd felt upon seeing her yesterday had melted away to form a warmth that circled his heart. The sensation both confused him and encouraged his next words.

"I want you to know that everything that happens tonight is an intentional act of intimacy."

Ethan moved his arm slightly, until his fingers found hers. She watched their hands became intertwined as if it were some type of anomaly and he waited until she once again met his gaze. The illumination of the candles gave her amber eyes a magical look, filled with specks of gold and yellow. Her skin looked like honey and was soft as silk.

"What's going to happen?" she asked in a quiet voice that went along perfectly with the candlelight.

"We're going to find some pleasure in this storm." Ethan wasn't sure if he was referring to the storm raging outside, or the one that had been steadily building within him since the moment he set eyes on Portia again.

"I think I know how we can do that," she said.

Her response surprised and excited him and he was about to ask how, but Portia was quick to show him. She moved so that in seconds she was straddling his legs. Now, Ethan was looking up at her.

"Let's take this off first," she told him as her hands went for the hem of his shirt.

He assisted her by lifting his arms and allowing her to pull the shirt up and over his head. Her palms fell to his bare chest and Ethan inhaled deeply at the warmth continuing to spread throughout his body at her touch. She stared down at her fingers as they moved over his pecs, the tight bead of his nipples and down to his abs. This was the moment where Ethan felt his hours of weightlifting and running paid off because there was pure enjoyment in her gaze as she looked up at him again. Passion brewing in the depths of her eyes, along with something else. Something Ethan wasn't sure Portia had ever felt before, power.

"Naked." She tucked her bottom lip between her teeth and released it. "We should both get naked."

"Ok." There was no other reply. He didn't know a man who'd ever turn down that suggestion when made by such a gorgeous woman.

They both stood, removed their clothes and then returned to

the sleeping bag. Ethan had pulled his wallet from his back pocket and retrieved the three condom packets he kept there. He dropped them on the floor beside the sleeping bag before sitting down again.

"Lay back," Portia instructed him.

He'd wanted to take his time looking at her body. He wanted to see every inch of her, front and back, from her toes to the nape of her neck. He wanted his hands on her, his mouth and his tongue…but she had other plans.

Ethan lay back against the pillows they'd propped against the wall and Portia pushed his legs open. He ignored the fleeting questions that popped into his mind as this wasn't a position he'd been in often. But she needed this. From the nervous sound of her voice the other night when she'd admitted to him that she was a faker, he knew she needed to feel like she was so much more. And he would gladly relinquish all control to her if it would take away that wary look she sometimes had in her eyes.

She was on her knees between his spread legs now, the dark circle of her nipples against her light skin an alluring contrast. Her breasts were high and full and his palms itched to touch them, but she pushed her hair behind her and bent forward before he could. Her small hand cupped his balls and Ethan sucked in a quick breath. She handled them as if they were precious jewels, holding them gently before moving her fingers over them as if she were actually cherishing what she felt. Tingles of pleasure rippled through him instantly and Ethan let his head loll back to rest against the pillows. He kept his eyes partially open, even though that was hard. He wanted to close them and completely immerse himself in the pleasure she was evoking. But at the same time, he needed to see her, to watch as he hoped she would find her own pleasure in everything she was doing to him.

When she wrapped her other hand around his hard length, Ethan released a low groan. She paused and glanced up at the sound and he watched as a combination of shock and encouragement flashed across her face. He lifted his legs so that his feet were now flat on the sleeping bag. She licked her lips and dipped her head lower. When Ethan thought she would have taken his dick into her mouth the way she had that dildo in the hotel, he was pleasantly surprised.

Portia's hot little mouth went straight to the sack she held in her hand. Her tongue lavishing the taut balls. He swallowed hard and gave in, letting his eyes close and the complete pleasure of her touch engulf him. Desire ripped through him in lightning fast shards that pricked every part of him. And when her tongue replaced the hand holding his balls, to rest beneath his heavy sac, Ethan moaned loud and long.

For endless seconds she kept her tongue there, very still as her other hand began to work his dick, stroking from the base up to the beads of pre-cum now covering the tip. His mind warred with his body. Was this better than a traditional blow job? Should he stop her before he exploded into her hand? Would it be better if he could explode into the warmth of her mouth?

Ethan would never know the answer to any of those questions as within the next few seconds, Portia grabbed one of the condom packets and ripped it open. She sheathed him quickly before lowering his legs and climbing on top of him. He reached up to grab her hips, but it was unnecessary. The look on her face said she knew exactly what she was doing and how she wanted this to go.

"It's all yours, baby," he murmured. "Take what you want."

With her legs now spread over him, Portia held his dick and positioned herself over the turgid head. She lowered herself onto him slowly at first, but then slammed down to take him all in at once. They both groaned with the instant friction and sheer pleasure that act caused.

She sat still for a moment and he watched with total enjoyment as she acclimated herself to him at this depth. Desperate to begin pumping inside her, his thighs trembled and he gritted his teeth with the effort of restraint. His hands moved from her hips to cup her breasts, kneading them gently, rubbing his thumbs over her thick tight nipples. She let her head fall to the side, her back arching into him. She looked glorious. All those lustrous curls falling around her like a halo, her skin so smooth and high-lighted in the candlelight. He wished he could snap a picture and keep it in his personal collection. This was pleasure right here, in the depths of her hooded eyes and parted lips, the obvious giving of her body as she simultaneously took his. Yes, this was a sight to behold and one that Ethan knew he wanted to see again and again.

Portia began to ride.

This was her first time in this position, but she knew how it was done. She lifted her head, leaned forward and planted her palms on Ethan's chest before moving her hips. The circular fashion was first. It made her feel his length embedded deeper inside. Then she tried up and down, so that a portion of him was leaving and returning to her in measured intervals. That pushed her need up to a roaring hunger. And when he grasped her hips, coordinating his pumps with hers, she knew this was how it would end.

The frenzied pumping, the increasing pleasure. The waves of desire crashing over her until she thought she would drown from it. Her breasts jiggled, her teeth bit down into her lower lip and she moaned. Damn, she was moaning as if there had never been anything this good, ever. And that was the truth. She'd never imagined sex like this. Not for her personally. Sure, she'd taught it and she'd believed that others could achieve this measure of bliss, but not her. It just wasn't meant for her. For this level of enjoyment there had to be something beneath the physical. Another connection that set the stage for the arousal to become so intense, so ultimately rewarding in the end. She wasn't capable of feeling like that about anyone, not ever again.

And yet, here she was.

Her legs trembled as her blunt-tipped nails dug into the skin of Ethan's chest. He moved abruptly and the next thing she knew, she was on her back, her ankles on Ethan's shoulders. He was over her now, driving into her deeper. She caught his hot gaze and couldn't look away.

"Unimaginable pleasure," he said through gritted teeth.

Portia recognized the words. She'd written them towards the end of her book. It came after the steps of intimacy and blossomed into a fulfilling sexual relationship. She shook her head, ready to deny that's what was happening, because that was impossible in this situation. But Ethan continued to move and while she could've sworn she was already at the pentacle of pleasure, he pushed her further. Pulling out and pressing into her from different angles now. Right, then left. Right, then left. He touched something inside of her, literally. His hard length scraped over the spot more than once and each time her heart beat faster, her gaze grew blurrier and then she fell. She was weightless, her mouth was open but there was no sound. She fell and fell and then she was flying, soaring.

Ethan groaned over her. He kissed both her ankles as a curse slipped from his lips. His hands tightened on her thighs as he pumped faster and harder, and then slower, in stiff motions that coincided with each groan.

"Unimaginable," he muttered.

"Not possible," she whispered.

He stopped moving inside of her. Portia's fingers gripped the sleeping bag, but then released it as her heart continued to hammer. He let her legs slide down slowly and pulled out of her after long moments. She immediately rolled to her side, feeling the warmth that followed when he pulled a blanket over her. There was nothing left to do but cuddle into the warmth and wonder what would happen next. This was not only unimaginable as Ethan had said, it was unpredictable and as her body came down from the inexplicable high of sexual pleasure, her mind roared with the unknown.

A few moments later, Ethan's arms were going around her waist. His body was pressing close to hers. There was more warmth and something else Portia never thought she'd experience with a man, comfort. Despite her reservations, she relaxed into the feeling, letting it and the sound of the wind and rain outside lull her to sleep.

Tonight, she'd had pleasure. She'd had what she'd written about and taught to so many others. She would let that be for now. And in the morning, she would pack her bags and walk away. Again.

12

A week later, Portia was still in Providence. As a result of the hurricane, most of the roads in and out of town had been flooded. The closed roads meant that Portia couldn't make it to the airport, which was just as well because flights had been cancelled the day after the storm until late in the evening. The call with her agent had been as pleasant as possible, all things considered. Her agent had been the one to break the news to the publisher. It helped that leftover rain from the storm moving north hit New York on Tuesday morning, so her appearance there would've been cancelled even if she'd managed to get there. Sadly, a few more appearances had also needed to be cancelled, but she was trying not to think of how pissed her publisher might be at this point.

There were parts of the town that also flooded, like Camy's backyard and basement. As for Sunnydale, the storm had broken a couple of the back windows. The glass shattering had awakened Portia and Ethan, and they'd gone downstairs to attempt a temporary patch job until the storm passed. But in the meantime, rain and wind had pelted through the plastic they'd managed to pin up to the windows and the walls and floors were damaged. Rod and his family business were swamped with repair estimates, so he hadn't been able to get to Sunnydale until Wednesday morning. Of course, he had a list of new things he needed to fix on the house now before it could be put on the market.

That meant Portia had to stay here. She'd made a commitment to Sunny, and her godmother had told her she was glad Portia was there overseeing the project. So, she couldn't leave until it was complete, not even to return to her book tour. Sunny meant the world to her and she wasn't about to let her down.

It surprised her to learn how easy that decision was for her to swallow, but as she recalled last night's impromptu gathering with Camy and her friend Rylan, she realized she could get used to being back in Providence.

Ethan was scheduled to work the late shift and wasn't set to get off until late so Camy and Rylan had stopped by Sunnydale with some of Jeret's famous hot wings, nachos and bottles of wine all pre-ordered from the bar.

"How many bedrooms are in this place?" Rylan Kent who Portia recalled seeing Camy with a lot when they were younger, asked. "Cause I'm tellin' y'all right now I'm gettin' tore up tonight! I've been working like crazy and my mother's been in a mood, so I need this release."

"Um, there're three bedrooms." Portia answered but she hadn't been expecting overnight guests and her mind wandered to needing to put fresh sheets on the beds. She'd stripped all but the one in her old room as part of the packing process.

"No worries," Camy chimed in. "We can all sleep right here. This couch seems comfy enough."

Camy and Rylan were sitting on the couch while Portia had taken a seat in one of the leather recliners across the room.

"And we can talk about my date with Steve last week." Camy

leaned forward and took one of the wings from a plastic container. She grabbed a napkin and sat back.

"Oh yeah, you said you were gonna tell me about that," Rylan said. She grabbed a paper plate and filled it with nachos and a few dollops of the melted cheese from another plastic container.

Portia wasn't sure what she was supposed to do at this point. She figured this was what they called a girls' night, but she'd never experienced one before. Because her stomach growled, she got up from the recliner and fixed a plate of two wings—the flats 'cause they were the best—and some nachos and cheese. Her glass of Moscato was already sitting on the table near the recliner so she sat back down after grabbing a napkin.

Camy had started her story and Portia settled back in the recliner to listen, eat and marvel over the concept of women sharing their private thoughts, laughing together and uplifting each other when necessary. That part had come when she'd mentioned the sad state of her personal life.

"I've been really busy these last few years so no, I haven't had time for friendships or romantic entanglements." That was partly a lie, but mostly true. If there'd been someone she wanted to be romantic with she would've made the time, but there hadn't.

"Your business is doing great," Rylan said, her words had begun to slur a little by this time, as she was totally serious about getting tore up. "And it's so empowering. I mean, you know women are usually shamed for being proud and open about their sexuality."

That didn't actually ring true for Portia because all this time she'd been focused on other people's sexuality, not so much her own. Until Ethan. Every moment she was with him she couldn't help but be super aware of her body and how it reacted to him. The last few days that physical reaction had shifted to something a little more powerful than she'd anticipated, but she'd chalked that up to all the fantastical dreams she'd had about him while growing up. She knew that now was different, that what they were doing was strictly about sex.

"Since you're so open about sex, tell us how good Ethan is in bed," Camy had said when Portia had been quiet for too long. "And don't leave anything out. Ry and I've been watching him and all Del's friends for that matter for years, and we've always wondered how they each were in bed."

"Yeah, we only wondered because Del and Lance would kill you if they even thought one of their buddies put a hand on you." Rylan chuckled.

Portia blushed. This was actually the real thing; it was a true girls' night and she was happy to be a part of it. Of course, that didn't mean she was going to tell them everything about her and Ethan, but she had shared a bit and it'd felt good. She'd also tried the hot wings and almost choked on the spicy hot sauce. Still, being with Camy and Rylan had felt particularly good and that had only been the beginning of their night.

So good that sitting in The Bullpen area of the bar today, she admitted that Providence was really starting to grow on her. With her laptop open on top of a small round table she sat in a cushioned chair facing the main dining room on the first floor. A half empty glass of Sprite and the plate which had held the tuna sandwich she'd eaten for lunch pushed to one side. She'd been here for the last hour working on the first chapters of her newest book and enjoying the scenery.

Ethan was on the early shift today. He was at the bar, taking orders, talking to customers and otherwise looking as sexy as ever. She lost track of how many times her gaze had drifted over to him and her mind had circled back to the time they'd been spending together. Since the storm, Ethan had been sleeping at Sunnydale with her. Even though Portia could happily attest to the fact that they did a lot less sleeping than one would imagine. The thought made her blush as her fingers hovered over the keyboard.

"Thinking of your next sex video?"

She jumped at the words, her surprised gaze immediately finding the slim woman who stood on the other side of the table glaring down at her. Portia's smile faltered as she stared into familiar eyes. And they were just as cold and dark as they had been years ago when Melissa Bannon sat two seats in front of Portia in chemistry class.

"Hello, Melissa," Portia replied curtly. She quickly minimized the screen on her laptop and sat back in her chair, hands falling to her lap.

One of her teenage nemeses looked almost exactly the same. Melissa's hair was still fire engine red, chilling green eyes still looking with judgement onto anyone she deemed unworthy. Portia had been tops on Melissa's list for reasons unknown. Melissa's body had matured into a svelte combo of generous boobs, yet her ass had received the same boost. Still, she looked fresh off the pages of a magazine in the fitted cream-colored dress and nude pumps she wore. A large leather boxed-shaped purse hung from the bent arm at her side.

"I heard you were back," Melissa continued, her tone just a hint shy of disdain.

"I'm not back." Portia felt the need to clarify. "I'm here on business."

That was true, even though there'd been a good amount of unexpected pleasure during this business trip.

Melissa dismissed that comment with a wave of her free hand. "Whatever," she said before flipping her hair back behind her shoulder. "I also hear you're into the porn industry." She gave a wry laugh. "I have to say that surprised me. I mean, Poor Little Portia, a sex goddess." Her laughter grew into high-pitched guffaws that caught the attention of two patrons sitting at the counter that faced the front window.

Immediately uncomfortable at the eyes that had shifted to her, Portia took a slow, deep breath and released it.

"Can I help you with something?" she asked Melissa. "Or do you have nothing else better to do with your time?"

The shrill laughter stopped and Melissa shook her head at Portia. "Still as clueless as ever. No, there's nothing you can do for me. Just as you're never going to sell that awful gaudy-looking house for anything more than chump change."

Portia tilted her head, raising a brow in question. "Oh, are you a real estate expert now?" she asked. "I thought I'd heard something about you being unemployed."

As a recipient of gossip which often turned out to be straight lies, Portia didn't pride herself on listening to or repeating stories she heard from others about people. But Melissa had always been a different case. Besides, last night's girls' night with Camy and Rylan had opened Portia up to a whole other world of female politics. Especially when they'd downed Pink Starburst shots and went through the Providence High yearbook with a 'where are they now?' segment.

Melissa's porcelain complexion paled further, her thin lips pulling into a straight line. "I happen to be married to a very prominent businessman who takes very good care of me," she snapped.

Portia nodded and laced her fingers together in her lap. It was her only nervous movement as she sat with her back straight and chin up.

"That's wonderful," Portia replied. "I always knew you would marry well."

"Just as I knew you would never amount to anything."

"Not sure that's accurate." Portia clapped back. "Considering my company easily grossed seven figures last quarter."

She didn't like to brag, and she rarely ever talked about her business or the profits with others. That could be because of the small circle of people she actually socialized with, but whatever the reason, this was out of character for her. But Melissa Bannon had always put Portia on the defensive. The difference this time was that Portia had no intention of taking Melissa's crap lying down.

Melissa shrugged. "I'm not surprised at all. Sex always sells. However, it's still basic and crass. But then I guess that works well for you."

"Success works well for me, Melissa. How about you?"

"Look, Plain Portia," Melissa said as she stepped closer to the table. "You're still the same uncouth little outcast that you were when we were younger. Hell, even your parents finally had the good sense to disown you. I hear your dad is a big shot in the political arena and your mother stands classily by his side. Both without their only dismal daughter."

The words felt like sharpened barbs driving into Portia's skin. They stilled her tongue and brought flashbacks of that last argument she'd had with her mother, but Portia refused to let Melissa see that she'd expertly hit her mark.

"I don't beg for attention, Melissa. I never did and I never will. Now, if you'll excuse me, some of us actually have work to do today. You can go along with…whatever it is that you do to make yourself feel worthy these days," she said.

"Everything alright here?" Ethan asked as he came up behind Melissa.

The infuriating woman had the gall to smile as she turned her head so that her hair flipped sassily in Ethan's direction.

"Why Ethan, darling. No, everything is not alright. I was just looking for a seat and I saw that this one was taken by someone less than worthy of this great establishment you and your little friends have here. I mean, what would the Town Council say if they knew you had a porn star working here at the bar that they were so nervous about opening in our peaceful little town? I'm sure if I called my Uncle Murray, he'd have to call an emergency council meeting to get to the bottom of this situation and that might lead to fines and penalties, and maybe even the bar being shut down until an investigation could be completed. Now, I know you don't want that do you, honey? After all, you and your buddies are supposedly working so hard to mend your broken reputations around here."

Portia watched as with each sugary spoken word that fell from Melissa's mouth like venom angered Ethan. His eyes grew to a deep dark green, a muscle in his jaw tightening as he stood silently listening to her.

"We're open to the public, Melissa. And as long as our guests act with kindness and decency, we're happy to serve them. You think you can do that today?" he asked, his tone not changing at all to reflect the anger Portia could sense brewing inside him.

Melissa frowned. "Don't let the porn videos fool you, Ethan. I pegged you for more of a man than a sex fiend, easily swayed by vulgar blow jobs and sex toys. But if you make the wrong choice—"

"There's no choice to be made," Portia interjected. "As I said before, I'm just here on business. There's no need for anyone to change what they've been doing in Providence on my account."

"The sooner you leave, the better," Melissa spat before turning back to Ethan.

She placed a hand with narrow fingers and mauve painted nails to the center of Ethan's chest. "Remember what I said, Ethan darling. Choose wisely," Melissa crooned and let her hand glide across his chest before she moved away, leaving Ethan and Portia alone.

Only a few seconds passed before Ethan reached for Portia's hand. "Come on, let's take a walk."

She shook her head. "You're working. I can just get my stuff together and head home. It's no big deal."

But it *was* a big deal, she thought instantly. After the incident with Bobby and all the flack she'd received during her last year of college, Portia had sworn she was through with running from her problems. Especially those problems that weren't her fault to begin with. She'd packed her bags and escaped from Providence as quickly as she could twelve years ago, in an effort to get away from people like Melissa. Now, she wanted to be stronger.

"I'm on my break," Ethan told her. "And I want to spend it walking through the park with you."

Portia didn't argue with him. She closed her laptop and slipped it into the slim black case she had sitting on the empty seat beside her. That case had a long strap and she crossed it over her shoulders so that it now rested at her hip. She accepted his hand and they walked out the front doors of Game Changers into the warm afternoon sun.

She wore flat sandals today, with a jeweled strap that went through her toes and rested on the top of her foot in a cute fashion. Her beige shorts came to mid-thigh and the pink sleeveless top she wore was just sheer enough to make him want to rip it off her to get to the delectable breasts he knew were beneath.

Her hand felt warm in his, their slow and easy gait as they crossed the street from the bar and headed a block toward the small dog park seemed easy and natural.

"When I was little, I dreamed about having a dog," Ethan told Portia.

It was something he'd never shared with anyone else before. Talking about his childhood wasn't something he enjoyed. Stacey had known that and had never pushed. That was one of the reasons Ethan had let down his guard with her.

"I wanted something like a pitbull or a Rottweiler because

they were good guard dogs," he continued as they started down one of the many cement paths that snaked through the grass and trees.

In the distance, six other people were walking their dogs. A beagle, two terriers, a golden Lab, a Pug and a Husky. Across the street utility trucks were pulling up to a parking lot where downed electrical wires still hung from the storm.

"For years I felt like I needed protection, but none came," he said.

Her fingers tightened in his grip.

"I never felt physically threatened by them," Portia said quietly as they passed a bench and a large green trash can. "They were vicious with their words. Especially Melissa. But none of them ever came near me as if they were going to do physical harm. I know jiu jitsu. My godmother trained me because she said every young woman should know how to protect herself. I would've been ready for any of them if they did approach me."

Her voice was even and she looked straight ahead. There was a quiet strength to Portia Merin now. Ethan recalled seeing spurts of it when they were younger. The way Portia always kept her shoulders squared and her head held high even when Melissa or her friends were harassing her. She'd done the same today in the bar when Melissa approached her. Ethan had watched the scene from the bar. He was too far away to hear what was being said, but it looked as if Portia were holding her own. By the time he was able to get away and approach them, he'd heard that his assumption was true. Portia hadn't needed him to save her from Melissa's evil wrath, but Ethan had wanted desperately to protect her.

"I was never afraid of them," she said. "I just wanted them to find someone else to pick on. For just one day out of my life, I wanted them to look to someone else. Anyone else. The way my parents did."

Now she pulled her hand away and walked ahead a few steps.

"I know you heard what she said about my parents disowning me," Portia said and then turned back to face him.

He figured something had gone down between them. In the time he'd been with her, she'd talked more about her godmother than her parents. Ethan pushed his hands into the front pockets of his jeans and waited for her to finish.

"I was a disappointment to them from the start," she said with a shrug. "I still don't quite understand how a child could be born to parents who never wanted her, but there it is. I used to think I was special because surely no other children went through that type of hell. But when I left for college and met other people my age, I heard stories of all kinds of parents. I started to figure that maybe mine weren't so bad. They didn't love me, but they had kept a roof over my head and food on the table. They never tried to get to know me, never understood me, but they taught me how to work hard and to focus on my goals. So I owe them partially for my success even though my mother made it perfectly clear with the launch of my second video on YouTube, that she and my father wanted nothing else to do with me. I was never to mention their names or claim relation to them."

"Because of your chosen profession?" Like, Portia, he knew firsthand about having parents that sucked. And how to achieve success regardless of that fact.

"Because it was the last time they were going to allow me to go against their wishes. The first time was when I chose which college I would attend and what I would study. The second…the videos, was the last strike."

Ethan lifted a brow at her word usage because while her parents had quit at two, he had his own three strike rule.

She sighed heavily. "I'm good with their choice. There was never any love between us, only blood. At first it was scary how easily it was to watch my mother walk away from me. But then, I began looking at it as a fresh start. I left the old life of Portia Merin behind in college and I'm very proud of the new Portia Merin."

Ethan's chest felt tight, like something was attempting to squeeze the life out of him. He took a step toward her because he thought it might be the fact that she was still planning to leave Providence and a part of him wanted her to stay.

"I'm very proud of you too, Portia," he said.

A chorus of high-pitched barks disrupted their moment and they both turned to see that one of the tan colored terriers had escaped from its owner and was charging its tiny feet toward them.

Portia immediately knelt down, a huge grin on her face as she held out her arms and caught the bundle of silky hair. The barking immediately stopped as she held the dog close to her chest. Ethan knelt down too, rubbing the small dog's head.

"These are the silliest dogs," he said through his smile. "They don't do anything but make a bunch of noise and demand a lot of attention."

"I'd give him all of my attention," she said lifting the dog up so she could rub her nose against its nose. "And in return, he'd love me unconditionally. That's why I used to long for a pet. Because they didn't have rules for you to follow or conditions on how much they would love you. They just did."

Ethan's smile stilled and the confidence he knew Portia had was again clouded by the vulnerability he now heard in her voice. This had been what he'd sensed was bothering her all along. The pain she still carried over being pushed away by her parents. He despised Wayne and Judy Merin and swore to take Melissa Bannon down a peg or two the next time she waltzed her snooty ass into the bar.

13

*E*than's loft was neat as she entered it two nights later. His furnishings were sparse and there were no knick-knacks on tables or pictures on the walls. There was a plush dove gray rug in the center of his living room space. She'd taken off her shoes so that she could bury her toes in it while surveying his extensive movie and music collection.

In this digital age, Portia was shocked to see that he had CDs lined neatly on four of the six built-in shelves on one side of the large flat screen television that hung in the center of the living room wall. He kept them in alphabetical order. The movies, however, were in order according to genre. Action, Westerns and Sci-Fi. She smiled when she saw a familiar case.

"Oh wow, you're a Star Wars fan too!" she exclaimed.

Ethan looked up from the island in the center of the kitchen. The completely open floor plan and lack of furniture caused an echo throughout the space, but was consistent with the contemporary look of the building.

"Of course. All the cool kids are," Ethan joked.

He'd been doing that a lot in the past few days. Actually, it seemed they'd both relaxed into a comfortable existence. Which was why she hadn't hesitated when he invited her to his loft for a replacement dinner. He'd wanted to make it up to her for burning the grilled cheese sandwiches the night of the hurricane. She'd offered to cook, but he'd insisted he could prepare something edible. From the scents wafting in the air, she was beginning to believe he could.

"Pick out your favorite. I'm almost done here so we can watch while we eat," he yelled from the kitchen after they'd been there for half an hour.

She got up from the couch where she'd been sitting and went to the shelf again, quickly pulling a case from many. She'd found the remote control to the television a while ago on one of the sleek metal tables beside the black cushioned sofa. Ethan came into the living room area then. He moved past her and came back with two small tables. He unfolded both, sitting them in front of the chair while she opened the case and inserted the disk into the Blu Ray player.

A comfortable existence indeed.

Minutes later Ethan called from the kitchen again. "All done. Can you come get our drinks?"

"Sure." She walked into the kitchen to pick up the bottle of beer and glass of Sprite he'd poured for her.

She tried not to feel any kind of way about the fact that he remembered she liked Sprite. He was a bartender after all.

"You made spaghetti and meatballs?" she asked after glancing at the two plates he carried into the living room.

"Yes. I did."

"All by yourself?"

When he turned, giving her a mock hurt look, she chuckled.

"What? It's a valid question. I mean, I watched you destroy two slices of bread and cheese, and this looks and smells amazing."

"I have garlic bread too, with freshly made garlic butter. It's warming in the over. Be right back."

Before he left, he dropped a kiss on her forehead. Portia smiled at how much she liked that small gesture. She also sat down on the couch in front of one of the tables. In seconds Ethan was back with the bread, setting two slices on each of their tables.

"Start the movie," he told her.

After she pressed the start button on the remote, Ethan grabbed her hand and she looked over to see that he was bowing his head. She followed and they blessed their food together.

"You didn't ask which one I selected," she said when he took a drink of his beer.

"They're all favorites so it really doesn't matter."

Until the words came up on the screen.

"How did I know you were on my team? Episode IV is the best always and forever," Ethan said.

"Always and forever," Portia agreed and took a forkful of her food.

She moaned with how good the food tasted. Ethan smiled and his chest poked out a little further.

"Yeah, you can thank me later," he joked and forked spaghetti into his mouth as well.

They were halfway through the movie and stuffed from two plates of food and more bread than Portia ever wanted to admit consuming, when Ethan's house phone rang. He seemed surprised at the sound and looked over to the other end table where a cordless phone sat on its charger. After another ring, he finally leaned over and grabbed the phone. Two very stiff, but cordial, sentences later and he stood up, walking toward the front door with the phone in his hand.

Portia wasn't listening. She was watching the movie. Eavesdropping was rude. But he was talking louder than Luke Skywalker and Han Solo.

"Are you crazy? Why would you think I'd want to hear from you now or ever?" Ethan was saying.

Portia shifted on the couch. She curled her legs up beneath her and focused all her attention on the screen.

"We have nothing to say to each other, so no, a meeting is out of the question. And your baby isn't mine, remember?"

That last sentence caught all of Portia's attention and she looked across the room just in time to see Ethan pressing the button to disconnect the call and glancing up to catch her gaze.

"It's not what you think," Ethan said when he was in the living room again, putting the phone back on its base.

He knew exactly what she was thinking. Just like he knew saying it wasn't what she thought was most likely the dumbest thing he could've said, even though it was true.

Portia reached over to the far end of the couch where she'd dropped the remote control and turned the television off.

"We're not in a committed relationship," she said slowly while rubbing her fingers over the remote.

She wouldn't look at him and that made Ethan even angrier.

"So technically you don't owe me any explanations." She cleared her throat. "But I'd like one anyway."

She did look up at him then, her gaze pinning him where he stood. Ethan didn't like talking about his past, and he especially didn't like talking about Stacey and the horrible break-up they'd had. But what he didn't like most of all was that look of hurt he saw in Portia's eyes. And even if she wasn't hurt because they weren't technically in a committed relationship, he still didn't like the possibility of her believing he was the type of man that would deny his own child.

He scrubbed his hands over his face and dropped down onto

the couch next to her. "I haven't repeated this story since I was sixteen years old," he said and couldn't believe he was about to do so now.

He didn't need to tell her all of this. He could just say that he knew Stacey's baby wasn't his and let that be it. She could either believe him or not. But she wouldn't believe him and while Ethan accepted that this thing between them was temporary, he would much rather her parting thoughts of him be of a positive nature.

"My mother left when I was six years old. My dad said she couldn't handle being a mother to a bi-racial kid. I was a little older when it dawned on me that it had taken her six years to realize that she was uncomfortable with her son." He paused because no matter how many years passed the situation still pissed him off. "My dad was a drunk. From my earliest memories I can remember smelling whiskey on him. That's actually how I developed my roots in bartending. When dad was too drunk to get up and fix his own drinks, he made me get them. I was ten when my father hit me so hard he knocked me unconscious. When I woke up, I finally figured my mother had actually left because of him and not me."

"Ethan." She said his name on a sigh and Ethan shook his head.

"I'm not telling you this for pity. I'm telling you so that you know what I've been through and you'll know the type of man I am," he said. "When I was fifteen, my dad was fired from his hundredth job. I'd stopped counting how many positions he'd held and lost years before. He drank for three days straight. I came home from school and literally had to step over him passed out on the living room floor. Then one morning I woke up and he wasn't there. I thought he'd sobered up and went out to find another job. Later that day, I was called to the principal's office where I was told that my father had driven his car onto the train tracks and sat there drinking a bottle of Hennessey until a train came by and ended his misery."

She lifted a hand to cover her mouth and Ethan pressed on.

"That's how I ended up at the Grace House for Boys."

"Because you were then an orphan," she said quietly.

He nodded. "Fast forward to senior year in high school. I couldn't wait to get the hell away from Providence and all the judging eyes of people who'd known both my parents and decided I wasn't worth a damn because of them. I went to college in Baltimore and applied for the Secret Service immediately after graduating with a bachelor's degree in Cybersecurity. That's where I met Stacey Kennedy. We dated privately for a year. No workplace fraternization," he said when she looked at him questioningly.

"Then one day, Stacey said she wasn't in love with me anymore. It was an hour after I'd been demoted for the first time in my prestigious career. Later that night, I wanted to speak to Stacey in person, so I went to her apartment. My supervisor, who I considered my mentor, was there. He's the father of Stacey's baby. Not me. And I don't know why she called tonight out of the blue. I haven't spoken to her in months and I made it clear that I don't want to speak to her again."

And there were his first two strikes, he clenched his jaw at that thought. Speaking of them reminded that when Portia had first come to town, he'd sworn she wouldn't be his third strike.

Portia didn't say a word. She sat for a few moments just looking at him, before she got up from the couch and came to stand in front of him.

"I believe you, Ethan," she said. "And I'm sorry you had to go through that."

There was relief and then there was *relief*. Ethan sighed with the latter, feeling as if a weight he hadn't even known he'd been carrying on his shoulders had been lifted. Portia now knew the darkest parts of his past and she hadn't judged him, hadn't walked away or criticized him the way so many people in his past had done. The way he'd thought she'd do when they were teenagers, hence the reason he'd never told her how he felt about her.

He was just about to suggest that they get back to their evening together when Portia pulled her shirt from her pants and lifted it up and over her head. She unbuttoned the khaki skirt she'd been wearing and pushed it down her legs. She didn't say a word and Ethan realized that he may have said too many. But he was done talking and from the looks of things, Portia had the right idea. Conversation and movie watching was over.

He pulled off his shirt, undid his pants and pushed them and his boxers down his legs, grabbing a condom before pushing his clothes to the side of the floor next to hers. She watched as he sheathed his dick and then climbed on top of him, lowering herself over him slowly. She cupped his face in her hands and whispered, "I'm sorry."

There was no pity in her eyes now, but there was sincerity. She could relate to his family life just as he'd been able to relate to hers. Did that make them a perfect match? No. It didn't. This was no love match, or any other type of match. This was sex. She lifted her hips slightly and eased down over him once more. It was damn good sex. And Ethan was going to enjoy it, for however long it lasted.

So he pushed Stacey, his parents, pity and or apologies out of his mind and closed his eyes to the pleasure. He lifted his hips off the chair until they fell in sync together. Stroking each other in the physical sense, bringing each other pleasure and passion. That was all that mattered. It was all that Ethan wanted ever again.

14

*E*than had no idea how long he'd been in the other room working out. His loft had three bedrooms, one of which he'd turned into a home gym. That's where he'd come before sunrise the next morning, after he'd lain in his bed staring at Portia as she slept. According to her book, everything they'd been doing was building an intimate relationship. They were linking themselves together both physically, mentally and even spiritually. The thought had shaken him until he hadn't been able to lay still another moment.

So here he'd been for the last two hours, according to the timer on the treadmill he'd just stepped off. His chest hurt after the ten-mile run on the machine. His arms hurt after the numerous reps lifting two hundred and fifty pounds. His legs burned and sweat dripped off every part of him. And yet, that feeling of dread that had settled in the pit of his gut still sat like a ton of rocks. Ethan stood with his hands on his hips and tilted his head back. He had to get a grip.

She was awake. He realized that the moment he entered the

bedroom and noticed the rumpled sheets but no Portia sleeping prettily between them. Damn, she'd looked good in his bed, her hair tousled around her face, lips slightly parted as she slept. He'd touched her cheek, which was probably a little creepy, but he'd wanted to make sure she was real. And she was.

He headed to the bathroom and heard water. After continuing inside, he almost cursed at the sight of her neck deep in his soaker tub full of bubbles. The water was so hot, the mirrors in the bathroom had steamed. The Cowboys t-shirt he'd given her to sleep in last night was on the floor.

"Mornin," she said, her voice still a bit husky. "Hope you don't mind. When I came in here to use the bathroom, I saw the tub and couldn't resist. There's only the old claw foot tub at Sunnydale that my godmother refused to let Rod take out."

Ethan swallowed. "It's fine. Soak away."

She looked as if she were doing just that.

"You can join me if you want," she offered after he'd walked toward the double vanity.

Ethan placed his hands flat on the marble top and lowered his head. Everything about her was tempting. The sound of her voice, the sweet scent of the bubbles he hadn't even known he owned and just like when she was in the bed, she looked as if she belonged here in his bathroom, in that tub. If he closed his eyes, he could imagine her in his space all the time. Forever. Sucking in a deep steadying breath, he released it slowly and called himself all kinds of idiots before cursing quietly. In seconds, he was across the bathroom standing beside the tub.

"I'll wash your back," he told her, because if he stripped and got into that tub with her, he was definitely fucking her in that tub. Only it wouldn't be just sex this time, just as it hadn't been last night, no matter how many times he'd tried to convince himself differently.

She smiled and handed him a loofa sponge. Ethan sat on the lip of the tub. He leaned forward to dip the loofa in the water and she surprised him with a kiss to his cheek.

"I woke up and you weren't there," she said. "I missed you."

His gut tightened, but he still smiled. He liked the sound of those words falling from her lips. "Wanted to get a workout in before heading down to the bar. Today's my early day," he told her and held the loofa over her shoulders, squeezing so that water trickled down her body.

It glistened, bubbles sluicing over gorgeous honey-toned skin. She sighed and his dick jumped.

"I love soaking in a hot bath. These past few months have been a bit hectic with preparing for the tour and filming the final videos for the year," she said.

"Do you like filming the videos?" he asked and dipped the loofa again, drenching her back with more hot water.

"Not as much as I used to," she answered. "In the beginning it was sort of liberating. Now, while I still believe in the purpose and the lecture material that follows each demonstration, I'm a little tired of twenty-four seven sex."

Ethan groaned at the irony of her admission. "Really? Because last night you seemed willing and eager to go all night."

They'd moved from the couch in the living room, to the floor just outside his bedroom because they hadn't been able to wait. And then finally to the bed, where only a two-hour nap had separated the heated bouts of sex that had continued there.

Portia turned her head to the side, resting her chin on her wet shoulder as she smiled up at him. It was a naughty smile, full of mischief and passion. He loved that look.

"I owe that all to my new instructor," she told him.

He shook his head. "I didn't teach you anything you didn't already know. I just provided you a live specimen to work on."

She shrugged. "I think I like working with a live specimen better than solo demonstrations."

"Is that so?" he asked and despite his better judgment leaned closer to her.

"That is totally so." She reached up at that moment, wrapping her arms quickly around him before pulling him down into the water. Ethan cursed through his laughter and cupped his hand to the nape of her neck.

"You're such a bad girl," he whispered while moving his mouth closer to hers.

"Right. You've tainted me, Ethan Henley. I've made a complete crossover with you. And I think I like it."

Ethan liked it too, way more than he'd ever intended. He liked it so much better when his mouth was on hers, his tongue delving deep into the warmth of her mouth. Finding the strength to pull away from her wasn't easy. In fact, it was a sort of torture, but he was okay with that. He deserved it for daring to believe this could be anything other than what it was. After soaping the loofa, he bathed her from her pretty peach painted toenails to the nape of her neck where he liked to kiss and feel her squirm beneath his touch.

When she stood to rinse off, Ethan climbed out of the tub and removed his wet clothes. He used a towel to dry off quickly and then wrapped a clean towel around her before lifting her into his arms. Portia wrapped her arms around his neck.

"I could so get used to this type of treatment," she said as he carried her into the bedroom.

Ethan could get used to it too. Going to bed with her at night. Sex in the early morning hours. Rolling over and waking up to her smiling face. He could get very used to it.

He set her gingerly on the bed and stared down at her gorgeous body. When she lay back and spread her legs in welcome, he licked his lips and prepared to take another dip inside her waiting heat. But something stopped him. As if a giant cement wall had been mysteriously erected right in front of him, Ethan came to a standstill. He looked at her full breasts, the dark nipples that made his mouth water, down her narrow waist to the mound of low-cut dark brown curls at her juncture. Then his gaze came back to her face. Her gorgeous amber eyes were staring back at him in question. She wanted to know what was going on, but Ethan didn't have the words to tell her.

How could he make her understand that he didn't trust anyone anymore? Not his mother, not Stacey, and unfortunately not her. And if he didn't trust her, how could he even entertain the idea of keeping her? The war between his heart and his mind was proving to be an annoying sonofabitch and he closed his eyes, trying like hell to think of some way to make her understand that this wasn't her fault. That it was all him. He was a hot mess and he hated that he'd pulled her into his vortex of disappointment.

Instead, Ethan took a step back. He dragged a hand down the back of his head and mumbled, "I've gotta get down to the bar to open up. I'll catch up with you later."

And then he went to the closet, grabbed his clothes and found sanctuary in the bathroom. When he came out twenty minutes later, Portia was gone. Ethan walked to his bed, where he'd last seen her sitting. He picked up the towel that had been wrapped around her and lifted it to his face. Inhaling deeply, he could still smell her scent. His entire body tensed at the aroma. He hurled the towel across the room and cursed fluently before dropping down onto the bed and burying his face in his hands.

He was a hot mess indeed.

An hour later, Ethan walked into the bar. They opened at eleven every day and it was just about forty-five minutes after that, but the lower level had a good number of tables already full. Music played in the background, baseball games, MSNBC, a pre-game football game and local news were on the televisions. Shaun, a trainee Ethan had hired part-time from the bartender school he'd attended, was behind the bar. She looked to be managing well considering only Rod sat in his favorite spot at the far end of the bar, talking to another man. She was filling an order when Ethan joined her.

"Mornin," he said in a voice he hoped was a lot more cheerful than he was feeling.

She looked up from the glass of soda she was making and smiled. "Hey Ethan."

"Everything go well opening up this morning?" he asked while moving around her to begin his daily check of supplies behind the bar.

Ethan hated to run out of anything, especially when it became crowded. He liked to fill his orders as quickly and politely as possible, without too many interruptions and found the best way to do that was to be prepared at all times.

"Cool," she replied. "That delivery you were expecting last week arrived. I signed the packing slips and put them in the folder beside the cash register as you instructed. The guys took the boxes back to the storeroom."

Ethan listened and frowned. The storm had delayed the delivery so he couldn't be too upset with one of his main distributors. Still, that meant he'd have to spend some time in the stock room today. That would probably work out for the best since he didn't think he was in the mood to deal with too many people today.

"I'll take care of that first," he said. "Just let me review the schedule for the weekend. The local college has classes starting next week, so we'll get parents and faculty pouring into town in the next couple of days. And Lance has some band coming in to perform on Sunday night. We're probably going to need all hands on deck. Are you available?"

"Anytime on Saturday and Sunday after one. It's Family and Friends Day at church," she told him as she picked up her tray of drinks and moved around the bar.

Ethan nodded as he pulled out the tablet they used for everything in the place and moved his fingers over the screen to pull up the schedule. "Got it," he yelled out to her, briefly recalling the yearly event at the church. While at the House, the boys had been required to attend all Sunday services. It was the grown-ups' that were in charge, way of trying to cleanse the boys' wayward souls. Even though there'd been nothing wrong with Ethan's soul at that time.

"Hey Ethan, you got a sec?"

He looked up from the tablet to see that Rod was now standing in front of him and the guy he'd been talking to was right beside him. A slim, borderline skinny man, who looked to be in his early thirties like Ethan. He wore a blue and white Dodgers cap pulled low on his head, so that the wire-rim of his glasses were more visible than his actual eyes. He had a backpack on one shoulder and what looked like a small recording device in his hand.

"Hey, Rod. What's going on?"

"This is Brent Reardon. He's from The Wire, a national magazine. Came into town this morning to do a story on Portia and her big book debut," Rod said. "Imagine that, huh? Out little Portia a bigtime author and stuff."

Ethan knew that Rod had been overly impressed with the "and stuff" that Portia did. Once she started coming into the bar regularly people had begun to notice her and not just because she'd grown up in Providence. Rod had been overly excited when he found out who she was and what she did for a living. He'd thought it a push from fate that he was working on her house.

But Ethan had politely pushed his thoughts in another direction as he'd very pointedly told Rod that Portia was off-limits to him. His old friend had seemed to accept that warning in stride, but today his eyes were back to looking bright with excitement as he'd said her name.

"Reardon," Ethan repeated. He'd never heard the name before, but he knew of the tabloid rag called The Wire. "You come all the way down here just for a story about an author?"

From his days at the Secret Service when part of one of the investigations he'd been assigned to consisted of him tracing dozens of media outlets for information, he recalled The Wire's home offices were in Chicago.

"Yeah," Reardon said, using a finger to push his glasses up further on his face. "It's a big story. We're trying to get the scoop before she starts getting invites to the morning shows and stuff."

Ethan nodded. "One little book is making that much of a splash?"

"It sure is," Reardon told him. "Rod here tells me that you've known Portia Merin all her life and that the two of you are pretty close."

Ethan shot Rod a heated glare.

"I mean, you are, right?" Rod stammered. "You were helping her out at the house too. Boarding the windows during the storm and things like that."

The look he continued to give Rod promised the guy he'd deal with him later.

"Yeah. Right." Rod said slowly with a nod. "I should be going. It was good meeting you."

The last was said quickly before Rod turned and made a hasty exit. Yes, Ethan was definitely paying his friend a visit after his shift.

"So, do you have a few moments to answer a couple of questions about Ms. Merin?" Reardon asked when he and Ethan were alone.

"No. I don't." Ethan's response was curt, but he wasn't going to retract it, nor was he going to apologize.

"I just want to know what she was like growing up. What type of childhood leads to a phenomenal career in the adult entertainment industry?" he continued.

"I don't know," Ethan said. "I'm not in the adult entertainment industry."

"No. I heard. You and your friends opened this bar a year ago. You all come from different careers, one of the Greer twins—Delancey—was with the police department in D.C. while, the older one, Delano, went a step above to work for the DEA. Noah Jordan was a Hollywood stuntman. I was a huge fan of Rock Patterson when he was on the wrestling circuit. And Jeret McCoy's an ex-Army Ranger."

"You did your research," Ethan said. He didn't like that at all.

"I did," Reardon admitted with a nod. "You were with the Secret Service, so I couldn't find out too much about you. But that's cool. I'm really looking for your insights on Portia. Was she abused as a child? Is that what turned her into a sex goddess? Her father's in politics. I plan on speaking to him next."

"Don't!" Ethan snapped.

Reardon tilted his head and Ethan knew he'd just moved Wayne Merin's name up to the top of people this jerk was going to contact.

"Are the two of you involved in a romantic relationship?" Reardon asked next.

"I don't have any comments," Ethan told him.

Reardon nodded. "You drive a silver Yukon Denali, right?"

Ethan didn't answer.

"I've seen it a few times, parked in front of that bright house where I was told Portia is staying," the nosy reporter said. "A few times."

A muscle twitched in Ethan's jaw as he glared at the man.

"It's cool, man. You don't have to talk if you don't want to," Reardon said with a slow grin spreading. "Providence is a nice little town. And if there's one thing I know about small towns, it's that there's no shortage of people willing to give you all the details of everyone who lives around them."

"That's not what you want to do," Ethan warned. "Your best bet is to turn around and head out of town. Leave the people of Providence and Portia Merin alone."

Reardon took a step back and folded his arms over his scrawny chest. "Is that a threat, former Agent Ethan Henley?"

Ethan kept eye contact and never wavered as he replied, "That's the best and the last piece of advice I'm going to offer you, Brent Reardon from The Wire."

It was too early in the day for pink colored shots, so Portia had made a pitcher of lemonade and baked some of Sunny's famous chocolate chip cookies. She carried a tray with two glasses and a plate of cookies out to the porch where Camy sat waiting for her.

"Oh. My. Goodness!" Camy exclaimed when Portia sat the tray down on the small stained-glass topped table that sat between the porch swing and two white Adirondack chairs.

Portia met with Cynthia yesterday and since the repairs to the house were just about complete, the realtor had suggested Portia work on curb appeal to help boost the price for the house. Sunny had scoffed at the idea but gave Portia the go ahead to access one of her many bank accounts to do whatever was needed to get the place sold. Portia had accepted her godmother's approval, but used her own money to pay for landscaping and the new porch furniture, just as she'd paid for all the additional repairs after the storm.

"This smell brings back so many memories," Camy was saying as she grabbed a napkin and three still-warm cookies. "Rylan and I used to walk all the way over here after school. She lived just down that block and was my excuse for getting a closer look at Sunnydale and these fabulous cookies."

Portia bit into a cookie and had to moan herself. All of Sunny's recipes were scribbled in a tattered book she'd kept in the kitchen drawer. Portia now had that book in her bag.

"Cookies and lemonade," she said. "That's what she always served while I did my homework. Of course, she had Caribbean rum in her glass, but she would eat just as many cookies as I did."

Camy laughed. "Those were the good 'ole days."

"So true." They were good days. Despite everything that had been going on around town, she'd had good times with Sunny.

"You ever think about coming back for good?" Camy asked after finishing her three cookies and taking a long gulp from her lemonade.

It was as if she'd reached right into Portia's mind and pulled the thoughts that had been floating there in these past few days out for dissection. While Portia had been content to keep those thoughts tucked carefully away.

"Sunny's not planning to come back," she said and then shrugged. "So it's kind of foolish to wish for old times to return."

"Before my mom became really sick, she used to say that everyone in town was shocked that Sunny had stayed here as long as she did. She certainly wasn't like any of the other women in town," Camy said.

Portia shook her head. "No. Sunny always said the mold was broken, burned and buried after she was created."

They both chuckled.

"That's fine. I kinda think their time has passed anyway. You know, my parents, your parents, Sunny and a lot of the other old farts around here. It's our time now. We're the next generation and we should be making our mark in Providence."

Portia wondered if Camy knew that she sounded like a politician in the making. "I believe I'm making my mark, just not here."

"Even now, after you and Ethan have had the chance to get close?"

She should've seen that coming. Camy didn't mince words. If she wanted to know something, she asked the question.

"I've only been back in town for three weeks," Portia started.

Camy immediately interrupted. "You've known each other all your lives."

"Not intimately," she countered.

Camy chuckled. "Well, everybody in town knows the two of you are just about living together. And I for one, am happy about it. My brothers and their friends have gotten the short end of the stick long enough. It's time they started to find real happiness."

"But they all left here and found good careers. What happened to bring them back?" Portia asked the question she hadn't been able to bring herself to ask Ethan.

Camy snagged another cookie and looked thoughtfully as she took the first bite. "Life, I guess. I don't know all the details about the others, but I know that Del and Lance's situations got blown out of proportion pretty quickly and before either of them knew it they were right back here, the place they'd longed to escape from. If you ask me, it's fate. They all belong here, the next generation as I just told you. It's our time."

The conversation drifted to plans for a weekend trip to National Harbor where Camy and her girlfriends would continue to extend their hospitality to Portia. They could shop, see a show and hit the casino. Of course drinking would be included, a fact that made Portia laugh because she wasn't the best at holding her liquor. But it was nice to make plans like that. It was nice to consider herself a part of a group of friends. It was nice and it was scary as hell because once again, it all hinged on Ethan.

Ethan, who'd acted very strangely this morning and hadn't contacted her all day.

15

By Saturday, two days after she'd spent the night at his loft, Portia still hadn't heard from Ethan. She'd thought about him constantly. About whether or not she'd done something wrong, or if his distance had something to do with that call he'd received from his ex-girlfriend the other night. All of the questions had culminated into a decision to take action.

Sunnydale was ready to be shown to perspective buyers. Portia had signed all the pertinent paperwork with Cynthia earlier this morning. The stagers that had been hired to fill the house with furniture that was sure to make it fly off the market, finished at the house just after five. And Portia's revised book tour schedule had just arrived in her email box with new dates beginning on Thursday.

She climbed into her car and drove to Game Changers.

Portia had no idea what she planned to say to Ethan, just that she needed to say something. All those years ago when she'd left last time, she'd always felt as if she'd stolen away in the night. Too afraid to face everyone head-on in the light of day. Now, things were different—vastly different. If her time was up here, that was fine. She'd enjoyed the weeks of freedom and pleasure she'd experienced, but her life would go on. Except this time, she would be absolutely certain that this "thing" between her and Ethan Henley was over with once and for all.

With her bravado in place, a smile and a wave for Lance and Joy as she passed them on her way to the bar, Portia stepped right up to where Ethan stood. "Can we talk for a second?"

He looked surprised to see her with his neatly shaved low-cut beard and those startling green eyes that sometimes looked blue. Today they were more blue than green. Somber, she'd say if she had to give the way he was now staring at her a name.

"It won't take long," she continued when he looked as if he were about to make some excuse.

"Sure," he said finally. "Give me a sec."

She nodded. "I'll just wait over here."

"No," Ethan told her. "We can talk upstairs. Go on up. I'll be there as soon as I finish this order."

Apparently, they weren't going to talk down here in front of a bar full of customers. That probably made sense. It almost meant that this talk was going to be bigger than Portia had even planned. She walked up the stairs to the Sky Box private lounge area. It was dim up here since they apparently didn't have any private parties booked tonight. Portia moved across the floor toward the restrooms where she knew the light switches were. As she flicked them on, she watched the room become illuminated and smiled at the fact that she'd known where things were up here. She knew because she'd been here a lot in the little over two weeks she'd been here. She'd helped set up for another event that had taken place since her first time being up here with Ethan a week ago and she'd cleaned the area with Joy and Camy so they wouldn't be here all night.

"I've got fifteen minutes," Ethan said.

The sound of his voice interrupted her thoughts about

possibly belonging here with her newfound friends and Portia looked up to see him walking towards her.

"If this is about me not being around the last couple of days, we've just been really swamped here. College kids and their families are coming in and Labor Day festivities are getting ready to take place. It's just been really crowded," he said.

He'd stopped a few feet away from her, folding his arms over his chest as he stared at her.

"That's great," Portia said. "This place is thriving. It's going to be a big success in town, regardless of the Council's wariness. They'll never argue with the revenue the bar is bringing into the town. With Lance's idea to bring in entertainment, the hotels in the area will see an uptick in reservations. The souvenir and specialty shops down on Main Street will also have increased business. It's a win-win for everyone," she told him.

"You sound like Del and Noah. Each of you have an eye for business," Ethan said.

"I've taken a few classes over the years," she said. "I even thought about going back to get an MBA. I don't plan on doing videos or writing instructional books forever. But I do like being an entrepreneur."

"You do it well," Ethan said.

"I do," she agreed. "So, are we finished? I mean, what we were doing. Is it over? It's fine if it is, I just wanted to get clarification this time around."

He at least had the decency not to look startled by her question. He had to have been thinking about this being the topic of conversation. She wondered if that were part of the reason he'd simply steered clear of her the past two days.

"To be honest, Portia, I don't know what we were doing. I mean, it started out as one thing—us toying around with the ideas from your book. But somewhere along the way, that changed pretty fast."

She nodded. "It did."

"And I don't know if that was for the better. I mean, you have your life in Seattle and I have mine here."

So it was going to be a distance issue. That was understandable.

"You're absolutely right. Long distance relationships never work. Glad we had a chance to clear the air. I have just a few things to tie up here and then I'll be leaving." The bravado she normally prided herself on was shot to hell, so she walked away. Staring at him while accepting what they had was really over was a little harder than she'd anticipated. The really hard part was acknowledging that Ethan wasn't going to step in front of her to stop her from leaving. The last time she hadn't given him a chance. This time he was making a choice.

"I can't do this, Portia," Ethan said quietly. "I need you to understand that it's not you or anything you did. This is all me."

She froze when he spoke, then snapped, "Cliché. I expected more from you, Ethan."

Actually, Portia had just expected more. She'd allowed herself to believe that they were moving toward something, when she should've known better. "I don't want you to do anything you're not comfortable with, Ethan."

They stood for a few seconds in silence and then both looked up as they heard the footsteps running up the stairs.

"We've got a big problem downstairs," Lance said to both of them, but his gaze had settled on Portia.

She followed the guys down the stairs to an almost silent lower level. Sure, the music that always played at the bar was still going, but the television sets that normally played sports games or the news were now playing something else. Her name whispered in a male voice echoed throughout the room and for the second time today, Portia froze where she stood. She hadn't even made it to the bar yet but stood just a few feet away from the front door.

She knew that voice. She knew the words that were about to follow her name, just as she knew the scene that was about to appear on those many television screens.

Bobby Adleman chuckled as he directed Portia to, "Spread your legs wider."

Portia closed her eyes to blink but couldn't bring herself to open them again. It didn't matter, she didn't need to watch the scene because she'd been there when it was recorded.

"Just like that. Now, just give me a minute...ahhh, yeah... that's it, baby," Bobby continued.

There was a shocked gasp, a hand clap and an offensive whistle coming from the room. The sounds were magnified since Portia's eyes remained tightly shut.

"Yeah. Ahhhhh, yesssss," Bobby continued before his next words were abruptly cut off.

"Oh, dear, there must be some technical difficulties," Melissa Bannon chirped amidst a few complaints from the male customers in the room.

"Well, it's okay. There's a complete version of this video up on The Wire dot com. There's also a very interesting story about one of the stars of the video, our very own Portia Merin. I guess this video proves the age-old adage that a person could actually sleep their way to the top."

Her voice was like nails scraping over a chalkboard. No, it was like sand being caught in every possible crevice of your body even after a long hot shower. It was irritating and infuriating and when Portia's eyes finally managed to open, she immediately sought out the redheaded bitch through her tear-filled gaze.

Camy and Lance were on either side of Portia as she took a step toward Melissa.

"No," Camy whispered behind her. "She's not even worth it."

"The police are on their way," Del said as he stood in front of the bank of televisions with now blank screens. "Whoever was responsible for hacking into our system and uploading that video will be punished to the full extent of the law."

Portia's chest hurt. She was breathing, because surely death was too easy of an exit for her. Tears flooded her eyes, but she shook her head praying they wouldn't fall. She couldn't cry. Not here. Not in front of everyone, especially Melissa. That's what the woman wanted. That would be the perfect victory for her. So instead, Portia looked down at Camy's hand on her arm and then up to her new friend.

"I'm good," she told Camy. "You can let me go."

With a nod, Camy did as Portia said. Portia walked across the room until she stood directly in front of Melissa.

The woman wore a haughty smirk. She folded her arms across her chest and stood with one leg forward, her chin tipped up, daring Portia to touch her.

"You're so beneath me, you can't even see your way up here," Portia said evenly. "You think you've won something, but you've only proven how childish and miserable you really are. I've already endured that video being played for millions of people on YouTube years ago, Melissa. This small crowd here in poor little Providence, is nothing. The fact that you thought it would be is quite funny." Portia surprised herself by chuckling.

"Oh. Look how quickly your look of triumph turns to one of indignation. Can you do tears at the drop of a dime too? If so, I might be able to talk to some of my friends in the film industry to see about getting you a job," Portia continued.

"You filthy little—"

Melissa's words were cut short when two uniformed officers came to stand beside her. "Melissa Bannon Colefield," one of them said. "We need you to come with us."

"What? Are you serious?" Melissa yelled as she was being directed toward the doors. "You can't prove a thing, Del Greer!

You and your delinquent friends are going to pay for this! I promise you that!"

She squawked and complained the whole way out of the bar and a few of the customers actually applauded. Portia felt nauseous and as soon as Melissa and the officers were out the door, she followed.

Ethan watched her load another box onto the back seat of her car before closing the door. He stepped out of his truck then and met her where she stood on the sidewalk. It had already grown dark, but he could see her as clearly as if she were in a fully lit room. She was beautiful and dangerous and he couldn't let himself forget that.

Every second he was near her, all he'd believed he needed in his life to be happy was threatened. But he couldn't stay away from her. Not after what had happened earlier today.

"I was going to send you all a card with my apologies," she said when she noticed him.

She'd tucked her hands into the back pockets of her jeans so that she now looked as defenseless as she had back during their high school days. He knew now that look was a façade, there was nothing defenseless about Portia Merin.

"That's not necessary," he told her.

"Yes. It is," she insisted. "I brought negative exposure to the bar you've all been working really hard to build. That was never my intention and it's important to me that you, the guys and Camy know that."

"They all know that without you having to say it, Portia."

Del had been so sure of it that he'd immediately known that Melissa was behind the video being played and he'd singled out the part-time server that she had bullied into uploading the video to their system. The server was fired and Del fully planned to do whatever he could to keep Melissa in jail or at least tied up in legal woes, for as long as possible. Ethan wasn't against that plan, especially not after the threats Melissa had levied the last time he'd seen her.

He was, however, still a little confused as to what exactly had happened in Portia's life after she'd left Providence.

"I'm not a porn star," she said evenly. "If that's what you're thinking."

"I wasn't thinking that," Ethan said. Which was true. That thought had entered his mind for all of three seconds after the video disappeared from the screens. But there was no way the woman who'd admitted to being a faker had once been a porn star.

"And even if I were, it's a high paying and respectable job in the adult entertainment industry, no different from any other acting position," she said.

Ethan wasn't going to debate that fact, having seen more than his share of X-rated films while in high school and college. He was well aware that adult entertainment was a billion-dollar industry across the world, and he didn't begrudge anyone who made their living that way.

"Nobody is judging you, Portia," he told her. "You can rest easy about that. We're not the immature kids we were back then. At least not all of us. You've come to mean a lot to our little circle and I just wanted to stop by to make sure you were alright."

"I am," she said quickly. "Thank you."

She turned and had taken a few steps up the path to the house when she stopped. Ethan was glad. He knew there was more he should say to her, that he should try to explain, he was just having the hardest time finding the words.

"I'm going to tell you what happened, Ethan. Because I think you should know."

"Okay." He didn't know what to expect, only that he needed to know. He needed to understand what had happened to this woman who'd changed his life. "Do you want to go inside and talk?"

"No," she answered and shook her head. "I'll be quick about it and then we can both get on with our lives."

Ethan didn't like the way she'd said those words or how they made him feel inside.

"I began dating Bobby the early part of my senior year in college." She eased her arms around to clasp her hands in front of her.

Ethan could see her fingers moving but she kept talking.

"I thought we were good together. He was my first," she said and then cleared her throat. "On one of the occasions that we had sex, Bobby thought it would be cute to record us. He also thought that video should be shown to the world, so he uploaded it to YouTube without my knowledge. I was mortified when my roommate showed it to me. I was going to barricade myself in my room to escape the embarrassment. But Sunny called me that next morning. I don't know how she found out what was going on, but she knew and she wanted to board the next plane so she could whip Bobby's ass. I talked her out of that." She chuckled.

Ethan could imagine that reaction. He wouldn't mind getting in a punch or two with Bobby himself.

"But then Sunny said something that made a lot of sense. She always did. Among other things that were said during that hour-long phone call, she told me to never let anyone have the last word over my destiny. I thought about that for days. And then I made my first video. It was a blow-by-blow replay of the sex tape with Bobby, wherein I explained everything that he'd done wrong."

"You did what?"

She nodded and smiled. "Yep. I turned the tables on that

bastard and made him the laughingstock of the school. And for a few weeks, it felt really good. Then I was flanked by guilt that I'd turned into my own worse nightmare. So I was going to take the video down, but when I logged into my account, I saw that the video had over three million views in just those few days. I did some quick research on paid YouTube channels and wondered if I could do it. If so many people were interested in what I had to say on this video, would they be interested in what I said on others? Within a month, I'd done research day and night, developing a script, toying with the idea of using a fake name, everything. Then one night I just did it. I taped the video and I uploaded it, charging for each view this time. And that's how Pleasure Inc. began. Two years ago, I was approached by a literary agent who thought I had the perfect platform for a series of how-to books to go along with the videos."

"Your success came from a vicious act," he said incredulously. "You built an empire on the back of the fool who tried to hurt you." She was a fuckin' genius.

She shrugged. "I did what I had to do to survive. And I succeeded beyond my wildest dreams. So, that's what I plan to do again, Ethan. I'm leaving Providence to continue on with my life."

He didn't speak, didn't really know what to say. *Stay. Be with me even though I've been a jackass. Live in this town where there're still vengeful bitches like Melissa.* None of that sounded right. It didn't sound fair to her and all she'd fought to become.

"We had a good time, but I don't belong here." She continued because he hadn't spoken. "I never have. Say goodbye to everyone for me. I really enjoyed these past weeks with everyone."

She turned away from him then and started back up the path.

"Wait," he called out to her. "Just wait a minute. I don't want you walking away thinking that what we did was just fun and games. You just don't understand where I'm coming from. You don't understand—" And he was doing a horrible job trying to explain it to her. His parents had left him, Stacey had betrayed him and this woman who'd opened his heart again was leaving him. Yet he couldn't find the words to make her stay, couldn't get out of his head with all the negative thoughts to beg her to be with him.

"Oh no," she said when she turned back to face him. "I understand completely, Ethan. We're both messed up by our pasts. And while we were strong enough to pick ourselves up and move on, we still hold the doubt and fears that made us who we are today. It's okay, I believe in always learning from my mistakes. I learned that I deserve more than an idiot who would video me without my consent, and a fling that was based on words I'd written in a book instead of anything either of us admitted to feeling in our hearts."

"Portia." He tried again. "I never meant to hurt you."

"And you didn't," she told him. "You helped me grow. I hope I did the same for you. Goodbye, Ethan."

hree Weeks Later

Ethan stood across the street from the dilapidated house at the corner of Furley Street in Providence. He glanced with fondness at the fire hydrant he and the boys up the street used to break open on the sultry summer days so they could play in the water. The lecture from the fireman and a slap from his father, was worth the fun they'd had.

He heard a car door slam and then another, but he didn't turn around. He knew who was walking up behind him.

"So, what's up, E?" Rock asked when he came to a stop beside Ethan. "You called us all over here to look at this shack."

Noah jabbed an elbow in Rock's side. "He used to live here, idiot."

Rock frowned. "I know that, jackass. I'm just trying to figure out why he's here now. He hasn't come back down this street since we all returned to Providence."

"He's right," Del said. "What's going on, E?"

Ethan inhaled and rolled his neck. Rock was right, Ethan hadn't come back to his childhood home when he returned to

Providence. It was a part of his past that he never wanted to relive. So he'd simply steered clear of it. But three weeks ago, Portia had said something before she'd left him standing on the sidewalk alone. She'd told him that their pasts had made them who they were and that it was okay to carry a part of that inside them because it showed their growth.

He had grown since the years he'd spent in this house with his father drinking and physically abusing him. And he'd changed from that boy who was angry about his mother leaving him. He'd changed and he'd made something out of himself, it was time he gave something back in return.

"I bought it," he announced. "This house, the land and that vacant lot over there. I bought it all."

"What?" Lance asked. "Why? It's an eye sore. Nobody lives on this street anymore. It's a dead end, so there's not even traffic down here."

"How'd you afford this?" Jeret asked. "We all gave our savings to open the bar. I thought you were tapped out as far as free money to use."

"I owned some properties in D.C. I'd been renting them out while I was living and working there trying to offset the huge mortgage on my apartment. When I came back here, I wasn't sure what I'd be doing for income, so I kept the properties," he said.

"Good move," Del added with a nod.

"I sold them last week and with the proceeds negotiated workable terms with the bank to clear this land and build something new." It felt good to announce that.

He looked around at all his friends and continued, "It's going to be a rec center, so the kids in Providence have somewhere to go when home isn't safe. Not a jail or a house designed to be another means of incarceration for kids, but a place where they can go to express themselves and maybe learn a few life skills. To encourage them and put them on the path to success."

"Oh man," Rock said. "That's what's up."

Jeret stepped up and clapped a hand on Ethan's shoulder. "You're a class act, Ethan Henley. A class act indeed."

"I'm gonna need some help, so I figured you guys—"

"Absolutely," Noah interrupted. "Whatever you need. We've got your back."

"Always," Del said. "Always."

Lance nodded his agreement. "And because we've got your back, we feel we can be totally honest with you."

Ethan lifted a brow. "Totally honest about what?"

"In short, we think you're being an ass," Lance said and then turned to the others for their opinions.

"Outside of this really cool idea you've come up with here, yeah, you're being kind of a jerk," Rock stated.

It was Jeret's turn to add his two cents. "For the last three weeks, you've been a sulky jerk. You even gave up a couple hundred during our monthly poker game because your mind's not clear."

Ethan stared at each of them in confusion. "How is it exactly that my mind's not clear? I mean I've been working hard at the bar and coming up with a great way to give back to our community, and you guys are standing here giving me flack."

"We're staging an intervention." Lance grinned.

Ethan frowned. "You're not funny."

"I think what they're trying to say, E, is that you may have made a mistake letting Portia walk out of your life," Del stated.

"Are you serious?" Ethan asked them incredulously. "She left. Just like my mother and just like Stacey. I didn't tell her to go."

"But you didn't tell her to stay," Lance added.

"You've got to be kidding me!" he continued, stalking across the street until he came to a stop directly in front of the steps that led to the house he'd sworn to hate forever.

He paced back and forth, trying to push back the immediate

anger that had erupted in him at their words. They were out of line. Way out of line coming at him this way.

"You, Lance, are the last one of us that would beg a woman to do anything for you. Are you really suggesting I should've insisted that she stay here with me? And do what? What?"

Lance and the others had followed Ethan across the street, so as he'd shouted, Lance had stood toe-to-toe with him waiting.

Rock stood a few steps away, his arms behind him. "You ever thought your life was meant to be different, Ethan? Maybe all the bad things that happened to you were meant to prepare you for something good."

Ethan shook his head. "None of you believe in happy ever afters. We're all back here trying to make the best of the hands we've been dealt. There's no fantasy world we get to reside in after going through hell."

Del shrugged. "Not a fantasy world, but maybe just a place where we can have happiness. Finally. Kind of like what you're trying to create for the kids here in town."

Ethan swung around to stare at Del.

"That's different."

"Is it?" Del asked. "You plan to offer those kids hope and solutions, but you're not willing to put your ego and your stupid three strikes deal out of your mind, to go after the one thing you've always wanted. It's her, E. We all saw it the moment she walked back into town. You've always wanted her. You had her and you foolishly let her go."

"So now what do you plan to do about that?" Lance asked.

"Your book has been on the bestseller's list for a month," Sunny said, her voice brimming with excitement. "And now they've offered you a movie deal. Is it going to be like that other sex movie that came from a book that everybody was raving about?"

"No." Portia shook her head and laughed as she held the phone between her ear and her shoulder. "I think the plan is to be more like a documentary type production, with actors from the adult entertainment industry performing some of the things I wrote and commentary from couples who actually put my steps into play in their relationship. At least that's what my agent said after her preliminary discussions with the production company. We're planning a face-to-face meeting in the next few weeks. Even though I won't have control over what they ultimately decide to do, they're open to at least sharing their ideas with me."

Her agent had told Portia that was a good point to negotiate in the deal. Portia had simply taken her advice because this wasn't something she'd ever imagined would happen. Tonight, she was speaking at another conference in San Diego. This time it was a psychiatrists' convention where she'd been invited to talk about her theories connecting intimacy to cognitive human functioning. The invitation had sealed the deal for the new proposal presented to her agent and in addition to the movie deal, another book deal was now in the works.

Her professional life was on a fast and invigorating track. As for her personal life, well, that was once again on the back burner.

"I think I'm going to come back to the states for Christmas," Sunny said.

Portia had just picked up the jacket to her black pantsuit and was pulling it on. "That would be great. This is my last engagement until February when I have some Valentine's themed promotional videos planned. We can definitely spend some time together. Are you coming to Seattle?"

"No. I was thinking of stopping in D.C. to see Judy. I miss my old friend from time-to-time. I know you won't come to that little reunion, but maybe you could come back to the east coast.

This house'll probably be sold by then, but we could get a hotel and visit Providence. You remember how they did the town up real nice for the holidays? And the big party they used to have on New Year's Eve?"

"Yes, I remember," Portia said with a sigh. "And I know what you're trying to do, Sunny. The answer is no. Not because I don't love you and don't want to spend time with you, but because I'm not going back to Providence with the hope of seeing Ethan. That bird has flown the coup."

Sunny laughed. "Listen to you talking like me now. I guess I've whispered in your ear long enough to have something rubbing off."

Portia laughed too.

"Listen, I gotta go. But we'll talk soon about where we can meet up to spend the holidays together. I really want to make that happen."

"Then we'll make it happen. I'm mighty proud of you, Lady-bug," Sunny said. "Have a good event and knock 'em dead."

"Thanks, Sunny. Love you!"

"Love you too!" Sunny said before disconnecting.

Portia turned off her phone and headed out of her hotel room. She caught the elevator down to the meeting room floor and exited with her mind focused on what she would say. She had her trusty notecards in her jacket pocket, her phone in the other. It was show time, something she'd gotten used to over the last leg of the book tour. Did she miss girls' night with Camy and Rylan? Yes. And she'd thought about her failure with Jeret's hot wings on more than one occasion. He'd dared her to try them again. Portia kind of wanted to take him up on that.

She shook her head free of those thoughts and walked into the room to see that all the seats had already been taken. Everyone seated was waiting to hear from her. One of the conference organizers met her at the door and walked her to the front of the room. Portia stood behind the podium, and pulled out her cards to begin speaking. She addressed the crowd, "Good evening. Thank you for coming."

And then she paused.

There was someone she knew standing all the way in the back of the room.

17

"*I*f you don't mind, I'd like to share something with the group," Ethan said from where he stood.

Much like she'd been that day he'd stood in the back of another meeting room while she'd given a demonstration, Portia didn't know what to say. The crowd had turned to look back at him in question and the conference organizer stepped up to the podium.

"Sir, this is a ticketed event to hear Ms. Merin speak. If you're looking for another meeting, there are persons outside who can be of assistance," the older man said in a stern voice.

Ethan had begun walking down the center of the room where there was a break in the chairs. He was carrying a box in his arms and talking while he moved.

"I'm not mistaken," he said. "This is exactly where I want to be. I've been waiting all day to see Ms. Merin."

At this point the organizer moved aside and began speaking to another man. That man signaled to someone in the back and Portia figured they'd just called security on Ethan. She hurriedly stepped away from the podium, intending to meet him and get him out of this room before he could be arrested for trespassing.

But Ethan knelt down just as she came to the end of the aisle. He opened the top on the box and tilted it over until the cutest little Yorkshire terrier came tumbling out. It looked as confused as Portia and probably everyone else in the room felt for a few seconds before darting toward her, yipping happily. Portia knelt down and scooped him up in her arms immediately. As she stood, it was to see Ethan coming closer toward her.

"I was an idiot," he said. "I'll admit that for as long as you want. But what I won't do, not another day, is live without telling you how deeply in love with you I am."

Portia tried to catch her breath. She held onto the dog who was trying to crawl up her chest or out of her arms. Ethan stepped closer.

"You said we helped each other grow and I believe you. I had no plans to get involved again, to give any sort of feelings to another relationship. And then you waltzed into town. You brought back parts of my past that I wished could stay buried. You also opened a door that I don't think I could close now if I wanted to." She'd missed his voice. She hadn't known how much until this moment.

"I wish I could've loved you twelve years ago. I wish I could've saved you from everything you had to go through," he said and finally reached out a hand to cup her cheek. "But I'd like the chance to give you my heart now. My heart and this great dog that I figured you could name Dale. You know, after the Sunnydale where you were happiest. I mean, maybe he could possibly protect both of us. Sort of."

Laughter bubbled up from her stomach, as pressure and warmth floated throughout her chest.

"This is a great dog because he'll love us unconditionally. The same way I plan to love you, Ethan Henley." Her head was swimming, chest heavy with emotion and then, as if just noticing, she glimpsed all the people staring at them. "Oh, the audience."

Ethan had been about to kiss her, she could tell by that look he always got in his eyes like she was the only person in the room, in his world. She took a step back, clearing her throat before handing him the dog...Dale. "Have a seat," she told him. "Right here in the front row so I can see you clearly this time."

He grinned, took the dog and grabbed the box from the floor before moving to the seat. As she walked back to the podium, she recalled another time when she'd been in a conference room and Ethan had slipped into the back and watched. Her heart still hammered wildly at the thought of him watching her, listening to her words and knowing she existed.

They'd come full circle. The thought filtered through her mind just as she began with her speech. As a teenager she'd thought herself in love with him, but really, at that time she'd had no idea what that word meant. Her parents hadn't showed her much love and to be honest she wasn't even sure they loved each other. But Sunny had loved her and she'd been honest with her always. What she and Ethan had now felt totally different from way back then. He was no longer that lost young man trying to find his way in a world that was determined to cast him aside. It had taken him a while to find his footing too, but he had, just like she did, and now they were both here. She paused in her speech and looked over to him. Dale was crawling up his chest and he had to use both hands to grab him and hold him still. She grinned, so full of love and of something she hadn't had enough of before, hope.

There was so much she and Ethan needed to work out, where she would live, who would get to keep Dale, if they'd both travel with her on book tours and other work trips because now that she had them, she wasn't about to let them go. But all of that could wait. When the lecture was over and she'd answered as many questions as her brain could process, she and Ethan made a stop outside for Dale to handle his business and then went up to her room.

"You're brilliant," he said cupping her face and moving in until their bodies were flush. "Every word you said tonight, your books—" He paused and shook his head. "Just brilliant."

Bringing her hands up to his arms she looked into his adoring eyes and felt wanted, needed, cherished. "And you're safe, Ethan. Your heart is safe with me. I know you've been hurt and betrayed before, that you've been living with the threat of that third strike hanging over your head, but you don't have to live like that anymore." Turning her face into his palm, she placed a soft kiss there. "I love you."

He leaned in, touching his lips lightly to hers. "I love you." Their lips touched again and her arms went up and around his neck. His slid down her neck and past her shoulders, until they were wrapped around her, pulling her tight against him. Here, right here wrapped in each other's arms Portia knew they were both safe now, together, finally after all these years, they were safe and surrounded by love.

And Dale's cute, loud-pitched bark.

PINK STARBURST SHOT RECIPE

Camy, Portia and Rylan enjoy a girls' night with the help of Pink Starburst Shots. Enjoy this sassy hit of color for yourself!

PINK STARBURST SHOT
makes 1 shot

- 1/2 ounce vanilla vodka
- 1/4 ounce DeKuyper Pucker Watermelon Schnapps
- 3/4 ounce sweet and sour mix
- Ice

Combine vanilla vodka, watermelon schnapps, and sweet and sour mix in a shaker over ice. Shake until cold, then strain into a shot glass.

ALSO BY A.C. ARTHUR

OTHER CONTEMPORARY ROMANCE

**The Donovan Series, Donovan Friends, & Donovan Dynasty books
(in reading order)**

Book 1: LOVE ME LIKE NO OTHER

Book 2: A CINDERELLA AFFAIR

Donovan Friends #1: GUARDING HIS BODY

Book 3: DEFYING DESIRE

Book 4: FULL HOUSE SEDUCTION

Book 5: TOUCH OF FATE

Donovan Friends #2: SUMMER HEAT

Donovan Friends #3: WINTER KISSES

Book 6: HOLIDAY HEARTS

Book 7: DESIRE A DONOVAN

Book 8: SURRENDER TO A DONOVAN

Book 9: PLEASURED BY A DONOVAN

Book 10: HEART OF A DONOVAN

Donovan Friends #4: A CHRISTMAS WISH

part of the *Under The Mistletoe* Anthology

Donovan Friends #5: ALWAYS MY VALENTINE

Book 11: EMBRACED BY A DONOVAN

Book 12: WRAPPED IN A DONOVAN

Donovan Friends #6: ALWAYS IN MY HEART

Book 13: IN THE ARMS OF A DONOVAN

Book 14: FALLING FOR A DONOVAN

Book 15: DESTINY OF A DONOVAN

Donovan Friends #7: FOR ALWAYS

The Donovan Dynasty #1: DANE

Donovan Friends #8: THE WINTER WEDDING

* * *

The Donovan Dynasty

Book 1: DANE

Book 2: ROARK

* * *

After Hours Trilogy

Book 1: OFFICE POLICY

Book 2: CORPORATE SEDUCTION

Book 3: LAWS OF ATTRACTION

Bundle: AFTER HOURS TRILOGY

* * *

The Indecent Series

Book 1: INDECENT PROPOSAL

Book 2: INDECENT EXPOSURE

* * *

Rules of the Game Trilogy

Book 1: RULES OF THE GAME

Book 2: REVELATIONS

Book 3: REDEMPTION

* * *

The Carrington Chronicles

Book 1: WANTING YOU - Part One

Book 2: WANTING YOU - Part Two

Book 3: NEEDING YOU

Book 4: HAVING YOU

* * *

The Rumors Series

Book 1: RUMORS

Book 2: REVEALED

* * *

The Royal Weddings

Book 1: TO MARRY A PRINCE

Book 2: LOVING THE PRINCESS

Book 3: PRINCE EVER AFTER

Book 4: TAMING THE PRINCE

* * *

The Temptation Series

Book 1: ONE MISTLETOE WISH

Book 2: ONE UNFORGETTABLE KISS

Book 3: ONE PERFECT MOMENT

Book 4: ONE CHRISTMAS SONG

* * *

Fashion & Passion

Book 1: A PRIVATE AFFAIR

Book 2: AT YOUR SERVICE

* * *

OBJECT OF HIS DESIRE

UNCONDITIONAL

LOVE ME CAREFULLY

HEART OF THE PHOENIX

SECOND CHANCE, BABY

SING YOUR PLEASURE

DECADENT DREAMS

EVE OF PASSION

PARANORMAL ROMANCE

The Shadow Shifters (in reading order)

Book 1: TEMPTATION RISING

Book 2: SEDUCTION'S SHIFT

Book 3: PASSION'S PREY

* * *

The Damaged Hearts Series

(Shadow Shifters Spinoff)

Book 1: MINE TO CLAIM

Book 2: PART OF ME

Book 3: HUNGER FOR YOU

Book 1-3: DAMAGED HEARTS BOX SET

* * *

Book 4: SHIFTER'S CLAIM

Book 5: HUNGER'S MATE

Book 6: PRIMAL HEAT

Book 7: A LION'S HEART

Book 8: A COUGAR'S KISS

* * *

The Wolf Mates

The Alpha's Woman (Available as part of the GROWL Anthology and CLAIMED BY THE MATE VOL.1 Duology)

Her Perfect Mates (Available as part of the WILD Anthology and CLAIMED BY THE MATE VOL.2 Duology)

Bound to the Wolf (Available as part of the HUNGER Anthology and CLAIMED BY THE MATE VOL.3 Duology)

* * *

The Legion

Book 1: AWAKEN THE DRAGON

Book 2: CLAIM THE DRAGON

* * *

WICKED: The Desireable Witches

CONTEMPORARY SMALL TOWN ROMANCE (W/A LACEY BAKER)

The Sweetland Series

Book 1: HOMECOMING

Book 2: JUST LIKE HEAVEN

Book 3: SUMMER'S MOON

Book 4: CHRISTMAS IN SWEETLAND (coming soon)

ABOUT THE AUTHOR

Stay in touch with A.C. on the web!

Be the first to know when A.C. Arthur's next book is available!
Follow her at BookBub to get an alert whenever
she has a new release, preorder, or discount!

Visit the "Contact" page on her website,
www.acarthur.net, to sign up for her monthly newsletter.

"Follow", "Friend" and/or "Like" her on Facebook, Twitter,
Pinterest, Instagram, Tumblr, and GoodReads.
You can also find A.C. on Book + Main Bites
(https://bookandmainbites.com/acarthur22/bites).

facebook.com/ACBookLounge

twitter.com/ACArthur

instagram.com/acarthurbooks

pinterest.com/acarthur22

bookbub.com/profile/a-c-arthur

goodreads.com/acarthur

Made in the USA
Middletown, DE
21 September 2020